Praise for

The WEIGHT of a THOUSAND FEATHERS

WINNER OF THE AN POST IRISH BOOK AWARDS
TEEN/YOUNG ADULT BOOK OF THE YEAR 2018

SHORTLISTED FOR THE CBI BOOK OF THE YEAR AWARD 2019

LONGLISTED FOR THE CILIP CARNEGIE MEDAL 2019

'Conaghan is a sublime storyteller who can make the reader
hang on his every last word'
The Times Children's Book of the Week

'An emotional rollercoaster of a book, written with so much
heart it bounces off of the page ... A bold, life-affirming read'
Irish Independent

'A hard-hitting, heartbreaking tale ... One sentence after
another knocks the reader out'
Independent

'The characterisation is superb ... A remarkably brave story'
Irish Examiner

'Conaghan's lightness of touch and sense of humour shine
through this heartbreaking story, and each of the characters
lingers in the imagination long after the final page'
Scotsman

'Although it's heartbreaking at times, there's also tenderness
and humour ... The tremendous empathy with which
Conaghan writes about young people is impressive'
Irish Times

THE BOMBS THAT BROUGHT US TOGETHER

THE M~~OTHER~~ WORD

THE M WORD

BRIAN CONAGHAN

BLOOMSBURY

LONDON OXFORD NEW YORK NEW DELHI SYDNEY

BLOOMSBURY YA
Bloomsbury Publishing Plc
50 Bedford Square, London WC1B 3DP, UK

BLOOMSBURY, BLOOMSBURY YA and the Diana logo
are trademarks of Bloomsbury Publishing Plc

First published in Great Britain in 2019 by Bloomsbury Publishing Plc

A catalogue record for this book is available from the British Library

ISBN: HB: 978-1-4088-7156-0; TPB: 978-1-5266-0815-4;
eBook: 978-1-4088-7158-4

2 4 6 8 10 9 7 5 3 1

Typeset by RefineCatch Limited, Bungay, Suffolk

Printed and bound in Great Britain by CPI Group (UK) Ltd, Croydon CR0 4YY

To find out more about our authors and books visit www.bloomsbury.com
and sign up for our newsletters

To my daughter, Rosie

PROLOGUE

Pain

When he's jabbing the thing in and out of me, I'm like, you better speed it up here, buster, cos this is about as funny as sandpapering anal warts. There's no screaming my head off or curling my toes in ecstasy. Seriously, hurry up.

I don't swear, as I promised Mum and Anna, my counsellor, that I'd try plugging the old bog mouth, but this situ requires a top-of-the-range F word. No danger it does.

My mate Moya had gone, 'Lie back and think of Babylon.' Or was it Matalan? Can't remember. She'd done it a couple of times herself, pure expert on the matter.

Only reason I let him do it – apart from BECAUSE I WANT TO – is cos everyone else my age is doing it and I don't want to regret *not* doing it. I'll never get this time back, will I? So, I took the bull by the balls, flicked the Vs to the world and plunged in. That's not peer pressure by the way.

Nobody, and I mean nobody, tells me what to do or how to act. Well, maybe Mum does, but I make her work for the privilege.

Everyone knows the first time's horrendous; mean, are you supposed to enjoy it? Yet, some people are mad for it from the word go, aren't they? Not me. I'm shaking like kittens over a river.

Feel like a complete zoomer lying here; frizzy-haired sandbag with cheapo trainers. Eyes the size of dinner plates, sucked into the headlights.

I've blinked seven times throughout the whole shebang.

His hand cups his drill, which he guides towards me. I'm numb.

This numpty tries to start a chat halfway through as if a crap confab will take the pain or awkwardness away. I stare at ceiling stains, hoping his ink will soon run dry. I'm like, can you not see the stress I'm under here? You absolute male! Ordinarily I'm an idle chat champion, but this is a time–place issue, so let's tone down the bark and concentrate, for God's sake.

'OK, honey, that's you,' he goes, and pulls the thing away. I'm thinking, *Call me 'honey' once more and that thing's getting rammed right up your pisshole, sideways.*

Act of kindness: he wipes away the gunk that's running down my belly and fingers some Vaseline on me.

Done. Job complete. That's me all grown up. Branded. An adult. No going back.

I climb off the bed, proper mannequin-stiff in the nethers, terrified to look in case it's a complete balls-up. I count to ten, do the breathing exercise Anna told me about, then have a quick glimpse.

'What do you think?' he goes.

'Yeah, not bad,' I go. 'I like it.'

'What do you mean, "not bad"? It's class.'

He hands me a little square mirror so I can get a good gawk at my belly button area.

He's bang on – it *is* class.

'Nice,' I go.

'Nice?' Tattoo guy tuts. 'What's "MY" stand for anyway?'

MY cos you can't rely on anyone but yourself, can you? This tat's only for MY eyes. MY life. MY body. Not YOURS. Not OURS. Me myself MY.

'They're my initials,' I go.

'Oh, right.'

'Maggie. Maggie Yates.'

If I ever get a gold band on the finger it should be with someone with a Y surname. Although, I can't ever see myself and some annoyance sauntering down the aisle together, pure blinged-up. 'Love Is in the Air' blaring in the background. God, can you imagine me cutting cake? Thought of it makes me howl. Or vom. There's a ton of living to be done before I start pram-pushing around the streets. And living begins tomorrow, cos tomorrow Mags the free-school-meals scrounger gets to burn her uniform and Maggie the art-school student will arise from those Primark skirt and blouse ashes. How cool is that?

Best not to show Mum my new tat; can't stand the aggro it'd cause.

PART ONE

Grenade

Here's the deal: I'm seventeen, but not like those teen morons on reality shows. Got to wonder about their parents. Here's another deal: I don't have parents. Well, I *do* have parents. I'm not like Jesus or anything. I just don't have parents plural.

Apparently, my dad had a PhD in Arsehole Studies with a specialist subject of hopping on anything smeared in lipstick. He phoned once to ask how I was doing, but the line soon died and so did he. Tragic … not really. By all accounts, he drank his liver into a spreadable pâté. Don't care; not as if I remember beard-rash cuddles or night-time tickles, is it?

I'm sorted about never getting to play happy families, even if Anna keeps yapping on about how destructive it is. God, Anna, don't get me started on her; that woman was born with flowers sprouting out of her chuff. Every time I see her, she leans over, pats me on the thigh and says, 'How are we today, my lovely?' Who's the one who needs help here, people? Mum says her heart's in the right place. Anna's all right in small doses, like tiny ones.

I wouldn't say I'm Britain's Next Top Model, but I'm not exactly bin-lid material either. Loads of guys have wanted to get their mitts on me, mostly malfunctioned mind-duffers from school. Even one of Mum's sleazy ex-boyfriends told me he couldn't decide if I was a 'wee cracker' or one of those 'borderline ugly' girls. Either way he'd be 'willing to give me a punt'. Proper Prince Alarming. Thankfully Mum, who's gifted in the art of attracting pure dickheads, blew Jailbait Jimmy out after that. If you clocked any of them in town you'd seriously think they were out on day release.

Leaving school behind at the start of summer was joyous. I celebrated by tearing all my reports to shreds. Not exactly Oxbridge bound:

Maggie Often Defies or Refuses to Comply With Teachers' Requests or Rules … *Prison would've been better?*

Maggie Often Sets Out to Deliberately Annoy Peers … *I blame Moya.*

Maggie Often Blames Others for Her Mistakes or Misbehaviour … *Totally blame Moya.*

Maggie Is Often Insensitive to Classmates' Needs … *Moya would kill herself laughing at this. Totally wag her finger in my direction.*

Mum used to say I suffered from CBS: Cheeky Bastard Syndrome.

Any wonder? When I was younger, I lugged around all these crazy thoughts:

Banging my head off a kerb.

Being bundled into the back of a white transit van.

Bunging a toaster into my bath.

Every example is a cry for help; all I did is picture myself in situations where people take pity on me, fuss over me, love me. Bonkers stuff, right?

My childhood memories don't consist of play dates, cinema visits and Haribo. No, mine's much noisier. Crying sounds in competition with slamming doors still echo. Being shouted down about everything I did: spitting 'NO' or 'STOP' inches from my face. Rank breath, the lot of them. I never asked for sweets. Never asked if we could get the bus home instead of walking. An unzipped coat constantly drooped off my shoulders. That's my memory anyway.

Childhood, the reason for bad decisions made and havoc caused. God, totally irritates me. Had to be learned some-where, hadn't it? Waving at you here, Mum. Although she's a victim too; being a semi-skint singleton would drive anyone round the twist. We're close. Well, as close as any teenage daughter and her mum can be.

When the rotten shit happens, I curse inwardly, beat myself up about it. It's like you can't help your actions, as if your mind is wired differently to everyone else's. Always think that I'm an island: the way I dress; the music I listen to; the patter my brain discharges. Everything.

Now's the time to make something of myself though. And I'm going to. You can't be pulling that mad stuff when you're seventeen. No way. Coping becomes easier at this age, choices more considered … I think. And I am changing. I am progressing. I am surviving, Anna says so too. Important year for me; can't be like the pure piss-taker I was at school. I care about myself too much to screw up new opportunities.

Can you believe they let me into art school? Me! Mean, no job at the end of it, but being an artist isn't exactly a job, is it?

Even though it's tarnished by the big grey Moya cloud hovering over everything, I'm excited. Yeah, that girl went and chucked a grenade into the mix. Exploded us all to shit street. Jackson Pollock style.

Affected

'And how are we today, my lovely?' Anna goes, followed by three thigh taps.

'Fine,' I go.

'No, really, how are you?'

'I'm fine.'

'Do you want to talk about it?'

Why does everyone ask if I 'want to talk about it'? Would having a good old natter dramatically change things? Would it separate the shit from the storm? Would it slacken the vice in my brain? The chest press?

Loads of people think I blame myself, but I don't.

I don't.

I DON'T.

I try not to.

No way I'm taking the blame for that. Look, maybe one

day I'll want to spew, but not now.

'Na, I'm good, Anna, but thanks,' I go, all sarky-arse.

'Oh, Maggie, love. I feel your pain. I feel your reticence to discuss it.'

'Right.'

'I want you to know I'm here for you.'

'Great.'

'To talk about …' *DO NOT MENTION THE M WORD!* 'The stuff in here.' Anna leans forward, taps my left boob. I think she's trying to find if anything's beating. My *MY* tat's throbbing, battering my belly. Probably should've done it after our meeting. Too late. Don't even know why I'm here anyway.

'What stuff?' I go.

'The important stuff.'

'Right.'

'How are things at home?'

'In what way?'

'Well, how's Mum doing, for example?'

Why does she care about Mum?

'Hunky dory.'

'Are you able to talk things through with her?'

'With Mum?'

'Yes.'

I struggle not to burst out laughing.

'It's important to let people in, Maggie.' Anna's tongue scrolls her top lip as if she's just invented the theory: 'Penetrating the Great Barrier Grief'.

'I hardly let her into my room,' I go, 'never mind …'

'It's not easy being a single parent, Maggie.'

Anna says grief can manifest itself cos of a 'lack of parental cohesion' (cheers, Dad) and 'parental disconnect' (cheers, Mum). Prattling on about how it induces stress and anxiety; now she's sniffing info about Mum, like a pure gossipmonger.

And what's with all the single-parent shit?

'Being a parent to me, you mean?' I clench my eyes.

'That's not what I meant at all,' she goes.

'Maybe she needs a man – she needs intercourse from time to time, is that what you're saying?'

'Maggie!'

'I'm joking, Anna.'

I'm sabotaging; that's what I do. It's like something inside egging me on. *Go on, Maggie, fuck this up.*

She folds her legs and straightens her old-lady skirt. I've noticed she does this when new thoughts enter her mind.

'Is there anyone in her life?' she goes.

'Who, Mum's?'

'Yes.'

'Like a man?'

'Yes.'

'No.'

Then I cross my legs and straighten my knackered skirt. The pause *is* good for thinking.

'Maybe it is what she needs right enough,' I go. 'Some rich guy to come along and sweep her off her feet. He can buy my acceptance in Topshop.'

Anna smirks. She agrees, I think.

But I'm serious; if any guy waltzes in then he'd better have deep pockets. I have issues, remember. Honestly, it's exhausting being me all the time.

'Good company provides positive energy for the soul,' Anna goes.

And … I switch off.

All that soul and energy tripe gets right up my hooter.

'Positive energy connects us to happiness.'

'Yeah, so does having loads of money,' I go.

She purses her lips as if she's watching puppies being carpet-bombed.

Perks up her boobs.

Smiles.

She's so delighted with her tits; always doing something with them.

Stands up.

Goes to the window, looks at the sky.

All very dramatic and Anna-esque.

'You know, Maggie, it's important to discuss what happened with Moya.'

'Is it?'

'And how your grief makes you feel.'

'Na, you're all right.'

'You do know that the time frame and pattern of grief is down to the individual?'

'Meaning?'

'It affects each individual differently – it's debilitating to shut down your emotions from it.'

I'm not a liar by trade, but sometimes needs must.

'I really don't want to talk about it, Anna.'

'It won't help if you run from it, love.'

God, my belly is stinging the life out of me, or is it this sesh?

'Who's running?' I go.

'Well, this is the reason we're here, Maggie, is it not?'

Honestly, my belly is pure pulsating; maybe we can blab about it next time.

Or the next.

Or the next.

'Yeah,' I go. 'Suppose it is.'

Anna's patience is ten times that of all the apostles combined. She earns her crust. But sometimes she's like the CEO of the Stupid Question Society. Mean, of course all this bloody affects me. Course it does. Try living inside my head for an hour and you'll see.

Spaghetti

On the way home I'm thinking about it: grief counsellor? Really? She totally has the opposite effect on me. I'm feeling the need to gush the grief out of me by star-jumping in front of a bus.

I saunter past the chippy, triggering mad pangs of pickled eggs and grease; is there a better smell in this world? Mum's promised a special dinner before my first day so I don't even look in the spitting fryers as I pass. Hope she's got her *MasterChef* hat on.

I'm starving. Feet are sore.

I blast in. Beyond excited. I'd be happy with fish fingers and chips, but she's all about doing a Jamie Oliver thing. Maybe she'll let me have a glass of wine. Then again, I'd rather drink my own stomach acid. It'll be pasta; that's all Oliver's good for.

I can't smell food from the hallway. I hear a drawer being yanked open; the crash of knives and forks. Sounds as if she's trying to kick shit out of the cutlery, or vice versa. What have I done this time? Some dinner this is going to be. Totally blaming that twat Oliver.

I leave it a sec before going in. Ready to get the sparring gloves on.

Pot of water is on the boil, steam flying off. Stacks of dead teabags sit on top of dirty plates. Manky cups everywhere. What's she been doing? Hosting a junkies' tea party? I expected her to be stirring or chopping. Where is she? I want to brutalise something, show my annoyance. If you say you're going to cook up a storm, then cook up a storm. Don't create one. Don't bullshit. Mean, this was her idea; put a bloody effort in, woman. Stick some flowers out, flap on a tablecloth, crack open the fine tableware; don't have the gaff looking like a ransacked homeless hostel. FFS.

There's pasta in the water; at least she hasn't forgotten completely. It'll be overdone. Thankfully we're not feasting on something she's brought in from school dinners. Totally had my fill of gloopy, stodgy, flavourless leftovers. Pure rank. Even though it says on the pasta packet to boil for eleven minutes, Mum always gives it thirteen 'to be sure'. Spaghetti doesn't even twirl on the fork after thirteen minutes. Calls herself a dinner lady.

She's standing at the door, looking into the garden, puffing away. Taking these big, long drags; following the smoke as it dissolves into the sky.

She's obviously in a mood so I don't say hello or anything; don't care. Place reeks of fags. Food's bound to be delicious. She flicks the butt far into the grass. Stuff the environment, eh, Mum? Think she's secretly raging I'm off to art school and not trying to find a job in Monsoon or Tesco, fuming that I'm not contributing to the household float. See, she thinks I'm going to be spending the next four years colouring by numbers. Belter of a celebration this is.

She turns to come back inside the kitchen.

'Maggie, Jesus, you gave me a fright,' she goes.

'What's for dinner?'

'That.' She nods to the hob.

'Boiled pasta?' I go. 'Magic!'

'Don't start, Maggie. I'm in no humour for you today.'

'Eh?' I go, cos this is what Mum does at times; she says something that riles me and when I'm riled we battle and suddenly I'm to blame. Mean, I could go off on one about munching fag-infused spaghetti or the state of her misery chops, but I don't.

'What're you on about?' I go. 'This was your idea, to celebrate ...'

'Just sit down and wait for your food.'

'Sake.'

I tut. I sit.

'I don't have the energy for this tonight, Maggie.'

'Energy for what?'

'Just –' she opens her palms as if submitting – 'let's eat in peace.'

I pick up my fork, think about ramming it straight into her eye. When she's not looking, I jab the four prongs into my palm. Sore. But, honestly, not sore enough.

Mum sits across from me, rests her head on the tips of her fingers. The sound of boiling pasta doesn't muffle the huffing coming out of her mouth though. I watch it boil. Why is she such a total whinge bag?

'Mum.'

'What?'

'The pot.'

She dives up. Turns off the hob. Screams the word 'fuck' really loud, then fires the whole lot into the sink. Kitchen's full of steam, rising from the sink. Wish a genie would appear.

'You mental?' I go. 'What're you doing?'

'I forgot to put a sauce on. It's ruined.'

'Tomorrow's a big day for me, in case you forgot.'

'Oh, please shut up for once, Maggie. Not everything's about your needs.'

'All right, chill. Sake.'

'And please do not tell me to chill. If I want to be unchilled, I'll bloody be unchilled, OK?'

'Whatever.'

I'm not joking, the desire to pick up a chair is strong. I stand up like I'm about to thrust this fork up her nose. I hurl it into the steam, watch it flip around. Makes that noise. Soundtrack of my youth.

I glare at Mum.

'I'm hungry,' I belt at her.

'See what's in there,' she goes, pointing to the fridge. Her voice calmer. Good job.

Just as I expected, piss all in there to get excited about. Feel like scooping out some of her Philadelphia (Lidl brand) with my finger and shovelling it into my gob; see how she likes that. Actually, feel like salvaging the spaghetti from the sink. I smash the fridge closed.

'God, what's the matter with you tonight?' I go.

I can tell she's at a stage of loopy far beyond her usual level. She sits, does this massive sigh. Cups her mouth. And mouth-cupping isn't good, is it? I know that. She might even be shaking.

I sit again.

'Mum, what's wrong?'

Her hand shifts from mouth to eyes; she kind of pinches them.

'What happened?'

She looks at me. No tears. That's something at least. More sighing.

'That's me done, Maggie,' she goes.

'Done what?'

'With work.'

'Eh?'

'I knew it was coming. I knew. We all knew it was coming. Cowards. They could've at least told us at the end of last year, given us time to find something else.'

'Mum, seriously, what happened?'

She throws her head back.

'I got paid off today.'

'At the school?'

'Yes.'

'What do you mean, "paid off"?'

'There's no more work for me, Maggie. They don't need me.'

'How's there no work for you? You're a dinner lady, not a coalminer. Schools always need dinners.'

'Council. They've cut back on everything. If it's not cost-effective it's cut. And I'm one of the cut ones.'

'So, what does that mean now?' I feel like a complete moron for asking.

'Means I've no job is what it means.'

'Just get another.'

She sniggers, pulls a fag out of the pack and heads for the door again.

'Yeah, I'll just get another job, Maggie. I'll nip out tomorrow and get one, that's what I'll do.'

Sarky cow!

I hear it in my head. I hear it: *What about me? What about art school? Who'll buy me new clothes and supplies? What about me, Mum?* Obviously I don't say that; I'm not a complete selfish psycho. Can't ruin her big spotlight moment, can I?

I go to the sink, fish out the slithers of spaghetti. Lob in salt and pepper, a grating of cheese and it can't taste that bad, can it?

'What are you doing?' Mum goes.

'I'm starving,' I go.

'You can't eat that, Maggie.'

'There's nothing else.'

'I think there's some soup up there.' She nods to the cupboard above my head.

'This is fine.'

Her eyes surrender; she looks sad and broken. Nothing a cigarette won't fix.

'I'm sorry,' she goes, blowing some of her fag smoke into the kitchen. 'I shouldn't have done that.'

Yeah, well, you did. So, too late. But I'll give you a pass for tonight.

'That's OK,' I go.

But it's not OK, is it? I thought we'd be laughing and chatting about how buzzed I am; I secretly hoped that she'd have bought me a little gift: new jeans or a pair of trainers. Mean, a job's a job – you just get another – but you'll never be able to recreate this moment. Totally tarnished.

It's minging, like spaghetti seasoned with dust. After two sucks I bin it.

'I'm going to my room,' I go.

'Fine.'

On the way out I dip into the fridge and take the whole tub

of Lidl-brand Philadelphia. Low fat, so I don't feel too bad.

Cutbacks?

Fucking council.

Just when I thought things were looking up, Mum plunges us deeper into poverty. It's not her fault, but still. Looks like I'll be wearing the same tattered gear all year then. I'll have to stay away from bars, unable to get a round in. I can deal with people thinking I'm a bit poor (not really), but I can't have them thinking I'm tighter than a flawed facelift.

Plumes of smoke waft up past my room window. She must be pure chain-smoking her lungs black. God, imagine snogging that. I don't put any tunes on cos I need to hear every sound. I know she's too upset to come to me, probably wants to avoid a ding-dong anyway. No, she'll stay puffing the night away, slugging wine and watching dross TV. She'll do her thing; I'll do mine.

Why does life have to be so hostile all the time?

When you snap a Bic, you're basically creating a shard of glass: razor sharp and durable. I've a choice of colours; pluck for the red one. I crack that plastic in two and press hard on my arm until a tiny trickle of blood worms out.

Here's me thinking that it's only rich chicks, the lonely and depressed models who do crap like this.

I'm scarily close to doing a proper five- to ten-centimetre slice. It's unreal trying not to, but I just about manage it.

Rough time.

It isn't sore; weird, cos my pain threshold is a level below pussy drawers. Weirder still: I quite like it.

In blood I finger-write *MOYA* on my forearm. Rub her out. Draw *M* ♥ *M*. Erase. Christ on a bike, Maggie, people at art school will flip their shit if they ever get wind of this. Who wants to be associated with a whack head?

I imagine that Mum isn't wrapped up in her own melo-drama for two minutes, and we're having a confab about it:

'It's nothing, just a tiny cut,' I'd go.

'It's more than a tiny cut. Looks deep. What happened?' she'd go.

'Caught it on a rusty nail.'

'What's going through your mind?'

'Nothing.'

'Why didn't you come to me? Talk to me?'

'About what?'

'You being truthful?'

'With?'

'The nail thing?'

'It's the God's honest.'

'You know, you're doing really well, Maggie,' she'd go. 'Really well.'

'It was an accident. The pissing nail was sticking out of the gate frame, snared my arm. Next thing I know, blood every-where. Nightmare,' I'd go.

She'd give me the I-don't-believe-you eyes.

BIG, MINGING ELEPHANT-IN-THE-ROOM ALERT!

OK, here it is:

Hello, my name's Maggie, and I dabble in the dark art of harming oneself.

There.

Said it.

Whisper it.

Conceal it.

Hide it.

But, please, never mention it.

Especially not to her …

Moya

Try giving Moya shit and you'd have known all about it. No joke, pure trigger-tongue that one. Like my protective big sister, even though I'm two months older and could probably beat her in a scrap. Our school had resources for students like us: anger-management sessions, padded cells, water fountains, breathing apparatus. We made teachers struggle.

We sort of became pals on the first day of big school. Girl was a mad riot from the moment we met.

```
When: School, day one.
What: Science class.
Where: Up the back.
```

'That's my seat.' Moya stormed right up to me, bold as brass.

'No it's not,' I went.

'Pure is.'

'Pure isn't.'

'Off or else,' Moya went, doing this mental hard-nut stance, hand on hip.

I did my own nutter pose. The state of us standing there trying to make the other think we're psycho. Hilarious when I think back.

'Else what?' I went.

'Else you're getting it.'

'Get me it.' I stepped forward, hoisted up my chest.

'I will.'

'Do it then.'

Fist clenched, heart bouncing; this cheeky little slaphead was about to know all about it.

'Cow,' she chucked at me.

'Bitch,' I chucked back.

'Slut.'

'Whore.'

'F …'

'YOU THERE.' Shout from the teacher.

Moya turned.

'Me, sir?' she went, as if butter wouldn't have melted in her arse.

'Yes, you. What's your name, young lady?'

'Moya.'

'Moya what?'

'Burns.'

'Well, Moya Burns, I suggest you find yourself another seat.'

'But …'

'No buts, Miss Burns. There, now!' The teacher flashed a finger towards the seat directly in front of mine. Moya plonked herself down. Face like a road accident. Pure raging. I was like, *YES, one–nil Maggie Yates.*

Then, tidying up at the end, I'm minding my biz, thinking how boring science is, shoving things into my bag, when she aims her daggers at me.

'Want a picture?' she went.

'*You* want a picture?' I went. 'What you looking at?'

'You, why?'

'Well, don't.'

'Or what?' she went, puffing out her bee-sting chest.

I was thinking, *What's this fruit's issue? Is she like proper mental or something?*

I tried to stand tall again.

'Else I'll …'

'Do what?'

Everyone's staring at this stage; boys majorly salivating that two girls might have a ding-dong, knickers flashing everywhere.

And that was it.

I'd had enough.

Couldn't be arsed with all that 'or what' and 'want a picture' crap so I smashed my bag on the floor and threw this mad eppie rant about how I was going to stamp all over her head and send her to A & E. Moya shat a brick. Me too. My insides clattering like a knackered washing machine. I'd never dream of stamping on anyone's head so I was totally relieved when she backed down. See, thing about me is that I'm all bullshit and bluster. Mum's said many times that I'm a mouth-first-think-later girl.

After we retreated, everything went majorly bonkers; in our next class we were dumped beside each other. Brilliant. Teacher was this man giant in Geox shoes; looked like life loathed him.

'Pens out!' he bawled.

Moya put two pens on the desk. Probably nicked from the bookies. I couldn't find mine. I rummaged around in my bag, face deep in its mouth. Panicked. Must've fallen out when I slammed my bag on the floor.

'IN SILENCE,' Mr Geox shoes blasted.

I wanted to stick my schoolbag over my head and disappear into the darkness. I could tell that the little head-wrecker beside me was dying to piss herself laughing. I pinged her my glance, ready to sever her smile with my tongue, but Moya wasn't sniggering, she was pointing one of the pens towards me. An ink gun.

'Here,' she whispered.

'Really?'

'He'll kill you if you don't have one.'

I took the pen from her hand. 'Ta!'

From that day, that class, we became inseparable gal pals.

Crazy to think how some friendships can be created through war, isn't it? Take note, Middle East!

Moya wouldn't let anyone act superior around us. Girl knew the score; our situations mirrored each other's. In shops she'd go ape if she caught the workers following us, thinking we were about to fire a bomber jacket or pair of liquid leggings into our schoolbags. We tortured ourselves with stuff we couldn't afford. I might be many things, but shoplifter I'm not. Still, we screamed penniless so eyes were constantly on us. I'd hide into myself, concentrate on the fashion, shift suspicion away from me, but the bold Moya challenged everything head on; ambushed them with a rant about their clothes, hair, make-up or anything she could find to hack them down with, pouncing on any defect.

'You gawking at?' she went.

'Erm … nothing … I wasn't gawking.'

'Think we're not good enough for your shop?'

'Can I … ?'

'Think we're here to blag stuff, is that it?'

'Can I help you with something?'

'Yeah, you can keep your eyes and tiny tits pointed in that direction, OK?'

They usually did. Didn't matter if it was teenagers or people Mum's age, everyone got tongue-swiped by her. Except hot guys.

Moya made me feel secure and worthy.

I sort of needed her, especially at that excuse of a school.

Place was full of immature wind-up merchants; where cruelty came on tap.

Insults were lobbed at us all the time; harmless ones like 'tinker trainers' and 'Poundland girls' to more aggressive ones like 'scabby welfare-spongers' and 'smelly rug-munchers'. I stuck a finger in front of their faces; she always voiced up:

'Know something?' she went.

'What?' some prick went.

'I'm sure we saw your mum on a porn site the other night.'

'What're you on about?'

'What was it called again, Mags?' Moya was the only one who got away with calling me Mags. I shrugged. Did loads of shrugging at Moya's improv.

'That's it,' she went, 'Glasgow MILFs. Your old dear's got some major talent going on. Anyway, can't stand around chatting all day.'

Always drew laughter.

She (we) always won.

As we grew into our teenage selves, she loved spilling the goss about her experiences with guys. I was murder in that department, totally clueless. I wouldn't have known anything if it wasn't for her. Still don't by the way.

One time she took my favourite cuddly toy, little Larry the lamb, and splayed him in a crucifix position on my bed.

'What're you doing?' I went.

'It's time we had the birds and bees chat,' she went.

'With a cuddly toy?'

We looked down at poor Larry.

'Right, Mags, point to where a guy has touched you.'

Nearly died we howled so much.

It was important she gave any guy I fancied the thumbs up. Her opinion mattered. Told her I thought Matt Lenton from our French class was kind of interesting.

'Yeah, he's a pure ride,' she went.

'Think so?'

'Totally gash-foam material. If he chatted me up in a dark corner I'd definitely let him finger me.'

'Sake, Moya!'

This was her pal compliment; that's the way I took it.

Lenton turned out to be a dick, like the rest.

God, I miss the howling we did.

Coping

I clench my jumper cuffs tight against the palms of my hands, feeling dead young compared to everyone else. Smaller, paler, weedier. Bet I look ill to them. Well, I am part of the chips-and-diluted-juice class, ain't I? Sorry if I wasn't brought up on avocados and olives.

In the matriculation queue I try not to catch anyone's eye; the other students are clearly much cooler, with their shabby-chic clothes and intimidating confidence. My jeans hang loose and my jacket pure drowns me. And don't talk to me about my tatty trainers. At least I don't have a giant arse, small mercies. As I shuffle along, awaiting my student card and schedule, I keep saying the name Alexander Lee McQueen over and over in my head.

Alexander Lee McQueen.

Alexander Lee McQueen.

Alexander Lee McQueen.

He diluted his juice and wore cheap gear too, yet reached the top. Wasn't his mum on the dole as well? He was a beast, an inspiration. Hard work and talent is what you need, Maggie. Alexander Lee McQueen is my new muse. I need to channel his energy. Nutcase switched out his own lights too; doesn't blemish his brilliance though.

My student ID pic fills me with pride; I can't stop staring at myself, even though I look like a drugs mule. This pic lets me know that I've waded through the shit swamp and come out relatively clean. Basically, screams achievement.

I stroke my tat.

I'm given my first assignment, to be completed before the class starts next week. What, I actually have to do some work without any time to test the waters? Got to take a 'scene from a Shakespeare play and use it to inspire a piece that sums up your artistic vision'. Eh? I'd rather lick a dog's paw. Bet Alexander Lee McQueen didn't have to do this kind of guff.

That night I know I should be ploughing through famous Shakespeare scenes for my assignment, but honestly, who giveth a fucketh? How's Shakespeare going to help with anything? Suddenly my mind's hissing, *What's the point in doing this course?* Bad thought on day one.

I read job pages on my phone instead. Not for me. Who employs seventeen-year-olds with zero enthusiasm? Anyway, most of the jobs are shit. Everyone's looking for nannies or skivvies. Crap pay, grubby conditions. Think Mum's past cleaning rich people's crumbs. Tons of taxi-driver jobs; driving drunk pervs around night after night? Erm, no thanks. For everything else you need to have a brain the size of a watermelon. There are a few things that could test her talents though.

'Bar job here,' I go.

She doesn't even look up from the TV.

'Mum?'

'What?'

'What about a bar job?'

'What about it?' she goes.

God, it's like talking to a coma victim with a fag dangling from their lips.

'As a job possibility,' I go.

She crushes her cigarette into the ashtray. They should extend the smoking ban to houses. I'm calling it for what it is: a form of child abuse.

'Who's looking for bar workers?'

'The Mint.'

Mum scoffs.

'Wouldn't even step foot in that place, never mind work there,' she goes.

'It's just a job.'

'Why do you think they're always looking for bar staff, Maggie?'

'Erm … Cos they have jobs on offer?'

'No, because the Mint is a zoo.'

She lights another; smoke streams from her nostrils. No joke, it'd drive you to a sick bag. I scroll down.

'What about something in childcare?' I go.

'That's what I do every day now, is it not?' She gives me this brazen sideways glance. I tense my legs, scrunch my toes. Cheeky mare! She's lucky I don't stub that fag out in her ear. Suddenly I have two choices: attack or scroll. I'm only trying to help. I could easily rip into her about having enough money to buy those cancer canes, but I don't, do I?

I read on.

But let's get one thing straight, I'm pure raging.

'Job here for a gym receptionist.'

'Too old.'

I keep my eyes on the phone. 'Here's one in a sandwich factory.' Mum switches the TV channel. *Four in a Bed.* Seriously? 'Oh, wait … never mind, it's miles away.'

'Don't you think I've looked at the jobs page, Maggie?'

'Yeah, but …'

'I have. There's nothing for forty-something ex-dinner ladies.'

'Wow! Share some of that positivity, why don't you.'

'I've filled in all the online forms, sent my CV to agencies. There are no jobs around here, Maggie.'

'So, what're we going to do?'

'We'll cope,' she goes.

'That's it? That's what we'll do?'

'That's right. We'll cope.' She blows two smoke rings towards the ceiling. 'Isn't that what we do?'

I know she's talking about me; good deflection, Mum.

'Yeah, we cope,' I go, pushing my phone inside my jeans pocket.

'Right, can I watch this now?'

'Who's stopping you?'

It's a bad day when you're being snubbed for *Four in a Fucking Bed* and a packet of fags.

We'll cope.

Totally looks like it.

I look online at famous Shakespeare scenes. Glare at the words. Read them again and again. And I thought *University Challenge* was brain-melt! Honestly, may as well be Norwegian I'm reading. If ever they want to cure insomnia, look no further than this activity. Thing is, I think most teachers haven't a clue either. Bet Anna does though; maybe I could ask her what that soliloquy in act five, scene six of *Macbeth* is all about. As if I care.

Shit, it's Anna again tomorrow. She'll want to talk about my inner balance or some other claptrap.

Can't wait.

Singer

I want to throttle her. Pounce on her like a mad puma or something. God, being in a sesh on 'unresolved feelings' is like sitting through an are-we-nearly-there-yet? car journey. Anna's fruit-looping her head off cos she thinks my current state of being is to punch shit out of people if I don't like the cut of them. Normal behaviour, apparently. I'm moving from stage one to stage two. That's right, people, grief has stages. Some say seven, others say only five. There's loads on Dr Google that says it's all a pile of pish though.

Don't worry, Anna, the only punches I've been throwing are metaphorical ones, usually at myself.

She swishes through her office, flapping her arms around like the world's worst figure skater, to 'ease floating tension'. I sit, preferring to lure all *my* tension towards my arse region and down through the seat. She's delighted, pure hand-rubbing

40

her excitement whenever I go see her, desperate to wring that grief right out of my bones.

I'll never tell her everything though. Are you daft? I like to distract her with trivialities instead.

'Listen, Maggie, it's insignificant if people don't like the clothes you wear. Who's interested?'

'Me, that's who.'

'Well, I'm sure you see lots of people wearing clothes you don't like?'

'Yeah, like maxi dresses,' I go.

'Maxi dresses? I don't see them as being an issue.'

'Can't stand them, that's the issue.'

'You do know I'm wearing one now?'

Really?

Course I know; could probably camp in it.

'But you're not squeezed into it, are you?' I go.

'Does my dress annoy you?'

'No.'

'Does it make you want to lash out?'

I'm convinced Anna thinks I'm a complete psycho. She's almost dribbling at the prospect of me saying yes.

'No,' I go. 'It's those big women who wear them over their fake tans that gets right on my ...'

'Which makes you want to challenge them?'

'Only when they look at me as if they're God's gift to fashion.'

Happy to be talking about clothes and style as opposed

to 'unresolved feelings'. I spend the sesh clock-watching. Yawnathon. Think Anna just enjoys a good chinwag now and again. She'd talk the hind legs off the Grand National line-up. Not sure if this is a grief-counselling tactic. If so, I'm on to her.

'OK, we've come to time,' she goes, which means we have two minutes at the end of the sesh for 'silent recap' (recrap). Anna's moment to sit with her lids down and breathe loudly. I'm supposed to do the same.

'Let's silently recap.' She shuts her eyes.

I close mine tight. Think deeply.

C'mon, Maggie, deeper.

Try to reach her.

C'mon, Maggie, deeper than that.

Try to find her.

Deeper, Maggie, FFS.

Deep …

And then she appears; an apparition decked out in Primark. Face beaming.

Back to that time it was all clouds and candy for her:

'You should see him, Mags, he's a total babe,' she went.

'Aren't they all?' I went.

'He can drive but he's not got a car yet – he borrows his cousin's sometimes. Said he'll take me up Loch Lomond in it one day.'

'Bet he will.'

'It's a silver one.'

'What, his tongue?'

'The car!'

'I don't get it, Moya ...'

'What?'

'So, you met on Instagram?'

'Well, yes and no. He's related to one of my neighbours – the one who's got the car.'

'Handy.'

'He commented on some of my Insta stories, then he posted some of his tats, then we started WhatsApping, then I sent him some photos, then we arranged to meet. So we met. He's dead nice, Mags.'

'Wait ... what, you sent him photos?' I went.

'Only two.'

'Of what?'

'Just a half boob and knickers, nothing major – it was only the top of the knickers and a bit of nipple.'

'Fuck sake, Moya. I'm pure mortos for you.'

'Calm it! I didn't put my face to them.'

'Brave woman, that's all I'm saying.'

'He's not a dick.'

'That's not a virtue.'

'It's just fun, Mags. That's what we're supposed to be doing at this age.'

'So, you actually met?'

'Twice.'

'God, your face! You've done it with him, haven't you?'

'Twice.'

'Moya!'

'What?'

'You could play a tiny bit hard to get.'

'Then I don't get what I want, do I?'

'Yeah, but, you know, there's easy and there's effortless.'

'OK, Mother Superior.'

'Just saying.'

'Yeah, well …'

'What does he do?'

'He just left school last year. Says he's got a few things up his sleeve. But he's always loaded and wears really cool gear. You should see his trainers.'

'You sound pure loved-up, Moya,' I went.

She grinned, fluttered her lashes. OK, so he might not have been a dick, but he failed the Instagram perv test with distinction. Mean, who posts their tats to teenagers?

I was happy for her, I was. Just hard to feel crazy joy for your mate who's out riding rings around herself, butter-legging it on date one.

When I reopen my eyes reality kicks in again, Anna's staring at me, mouth wide. She nods her head. And suddenly we're meant to feel better.

I don't.

Oh, see that little art-school Shakespeare assignment? Well, turns out it isn't so little after all; more purgatory than assignment. Got to be done in collaboration, in groups of four. Gone is the notion of Me, My, I. Now it's Us, Our, We, and I'm locked into a WhatsApp gaggle with a bunch of outsiders. Magic! Talk about stranger danger.

You can just tell from their names that we don't swing from the same monkey bars. I'd wager that Alfie and Davis each had their own playroom growing up, which became a den, then a study zone and now, most likely, a wanking wing. And, don't laugh, but there's someone called Plum. Unsure of the gender. Very sure the parents are a right couple of twartists though. Mean, what kind of child abusers call their kid after an easily bruised fruit?

Davis messaged the group suggesting we all meet up to talk about the assignment. Where do you think he suggested?

Library? Wrong.

Art school studio? No.

Bar? Fat chance.

No, this Davis person suggested we all meet in the foyer of Cineworld. I know, right? My knob-alert siren is blaring. Apparently, he and Alfie want to go watch some dick-flick later.

So after the head-clamping sesh with Anna, I hot-step it to Cineworld with all the zeal of an escort who's off to see Big Bob the Banker. I wear my *Hatful of Hollow* T-shirt and cardie to look more studenty and, also, to hide my cash-flow situation. Doubt they'll be into the Smiths anyway.

The three of them are sitting around a table, chatting away

like they're old friends. I recognise the two guys from their WhatsApp pics. Plum is female. The three of them are actually having a conversation and laughing. Like, really listening to each other. Weirdos. Maybe Moya was right about art school.

When they clock me, all chinwagging stops; their eyes lock, sketching me top to bottom. My chest wants to combust. I sense myself shrinking and want to melt into the ground like that green witch from *The Wizard of Oz*. Davis stands. I cross one foot over the other.

'Maggie?' he goes.

'Yeah,' I go, trying to sound cool.

'Great T-shirt,' he goes.

And in that instant, I fancy him. No Instagram half-nipple photo required, just one person standing in front of the other. Smiling, being normal. I flick my head and kind of girlie laugh. I'd punch myself if I could.

'Oh, this?' I go, secretly chuffed. 'Thanks.'

'These guys are Alfie and Plum.'

Plum puts her hand out for me to shake. I feel slightly embarrassed; it's as if we're playing at being adults. My skin's clammy. Moya's laughter rattles around my head when our palms touch.

'Hi,' Plum goes, very mousey, as awkward as me.

'All right, Maggie?' Alfie goes, saluting me. Actually saluting.

'Sorry I'm a bit late,' I go, sitting at the table. 'Have I missed anything?'

'We were just chatting about music and bands and shit,' Alfie goes.

'Really?' I go, eyes wide.

'See,' Davis says, 'Alfie and me have been talking about starting a band since we were small ...'

'You two know each other?' I go.

'Best mates,' they say in unison.

'Oh,' I go.

'And Plum's his girlfriend,' Davis goes.

Plum looks mortos while Alfie puts on a cock-of-the-walk grin; pure delighted that he's managed to bag a bird.

'Strange that you all go to the same art school?' I go.

'Yeah, mad, innit?' Davis goes.

My thoughts jump to inbreeding.

'Yeah, that is mad,' I go. They smile and nod to one another. 'So, anyone got any ideas about this Shakespeare thing?'

Silence. Confusion. Am I at the wrong meeting?

'I was thinking we could maybe look at costume design,' I add.

Alfie and Davis laugh.

'Naw, fuck that,' Alfie says. 'Let's talk about starting a band. A proper one.'

Plum purses her lips; think she wants to apologise.

'Really?' I go.

'Yeah, that Shakespeare stuff can wait,' Davis says.

'I'd love to be in a band one day,' I lie.

Well, half lie. It would be kinda cool.

'Wait,' Alfie goes, looking at the others. 'Can you chant, Maggie?'

'Eh?'

'Can you sing?'

'Erm …'

'Not a bad idea,' Davis goes. 'I mean, you're halfway there with that T-shirt on. Any fan of the Smiths is welcome in our band.'

'Totally,' Alfie goes.

'So, Maggie, can you sing or what?' Davis goes.

I think I can. I know I can. I'm good, decent. Mean, I can hold a tune. Mum once said that I should go on *The X Factor*. I know it was after she'd rattled a bottle of Pinot Noir into herself, but she was serious. *The X Factor*? Shove that.

'It might be nice to have another girl in the band,' Plum goes.

What's just happened? One minute I'm thinking Shakespeare scenes and costume design, trying not to come across as a thicko, and the next I'm being thrust into the role of lead singer in an unnamed band. Got to love life sometimes.

They're actually mulling it over, totally examining my body. Feel like screaming, 'Hey, I'm not here for a fucking modelling job.'

'I think you should do it,' Davis goes.

'Absolutely, you should,' Alfie goes.

'It might be an enjoyable experience,' Plum adds.

Sometimes peer pressure is so comforting.

This Davis guy wants to start a two-girl-two-boy band. Suddenly I'm thinking, *This could work. Me and three strangers, who've no idea about my baggage, could possibly function. An alternative therapy.* Is the universe trying to soothe me? Can't help but love that. Mean, who doesn't want to be in a band?

'You haven't heard me sing yet. I might be utter crap,' I go.

'She's right, you know,' Alfie says to the others. 'She could be tone deaf.'

'Tone deaf?' I go. 'I'm anything but.'

'There you go,' Davis goes. 'She's a chanter.'

'OK,' Alfie says. 'Cool with me.'

'I think it'll work out,' Plum adds, giving me the don't-leave-me-with-these-two-numpties eyes.

'OK, I'm in!' I go. 'What kind of band are you thinking of?'

'Like Take That after Robbie left, but with two girls,' Alfie goes.

'Take That are shit,' Davis states.

'I'm not a fan,' Plum goes.

'I thought you'd be thinking of something a bit edgier,' I go. 'Indie stuff.'

'No, we are. Totally are,' Davis says, slapping Alfie on the shoulder. 'Don't listen to him.'

'Edgy pop,' Alfie goes.

'No pop,' Davis says.

'I'm not a fan,' Plum goes.

'What do you play, Plum?' I go.

The lads laugh. Plum shuffles uncomfortably, as if I've just asked if she wants to have a threesome. Davis takes me through all the instruments in Plum's repertoire; she's like a one-woman orchestra – you name it, she plays it. Girl's a freak of nature.

'Right, so, we're not playing pop,' I go. 'Agreed?' I think they're taken aback by my brazenness, just waltzing in with my creative demands. Doing a pure Yoko. But what's the point of being a lead singer if I can't voice my opinion?

No one speaks.

'So, indie band then?' I go. 'Agreed?'

Still nothing.

I wait for a response, give them eyes.

'Agreed,' Davis goes.

'Agreed,' Alfie goes.

'Yes, fine,' Plum goes.

'So, no piss-poor pop. Only stuff with attitude and V-signs,' I go, reinforcing my point.

I've bagged my role of the hot, sexy, sweaty singer; Karen O from Yeah Yeah Yeahs springs to mind. Alfie's on drums; exactly where you stick those with shadows on their brain, isn't it? Jury's still out on Alfie in that regard. Davis is on guitar; he can play lots of Beatles and Smiths songs, but insultingly bad, apparently. Plum will be left to do everything else: bass, piano bits and strings. I'm glad to be the singer. Can't afford an instrument, nor can I play one.

50

Everyone's forgotten about Shakespeare scenes and art school assignments. It's good being a full-time student.

'What are we going to call this band?' I go.

'I've been thinking about this,' Alfie goes. We prick up. 'What about Four Tops?'

'I think that band already exists,' Plum states.

'Four Seasons then?' Alfie adds.

'Like the hotel?' Davis goes.

'If I can just say,' Plum pipes, 'I think that band name also exists.'

'And what's with all the numbers?' I go.

'Stop!' Davis booms, putting his hand in the air. 'Maybe next meeting each person has to come with at least one potential band name.'

'Agreed,' I go.

'Agreed,' Alfie goes.

'Yes, fine,' Plum goes.

'And it has to start with *the* something,' Davis adds.

'Agreed?' we all go.

We talk so much that Davis and Alfie miss their dick-flick. I care zero per cent.

It's pissing down. We huddle in a bus shelter outside Cineworld. Alfie and Plum sit on the metal bench, knees and fingers touching. I try not to watch. Feel like a complete gooseberry. I sort of give Davis a toothy grin. He smiles. We say nothing, like our lips are sewn up. I'd walk the discomfort away if it wasn't belting it down. Alfie and Plum peck each other. God!

I stare straight ahead and imagine snogging Davis; imagine hooking my arms around his waist, him fixing his around mine. He puts his tongue in my mouth, more than the tip. I'm not mad on exhibition kissing, but I go with it. Enjoy it. No, love it.

Everything is so wet; I despise rain.

When my bus arrives, I sneak on through the back doors. Heart chugging all the way home. White-knuckle ride.

Chippy

I've a major spring in my step, dead excited about telling Mum I'm going to be the cool singer in a band. How in a few years I might be able to buy her a better gaff or whisk her away to the sun or get her fashionable clothes. Can't wait to put a smile on her chops, make her proud of me for doing something other than darkening her door.

I practically sprint from the bus stop.

'Mum, guess what?' I shout as soon as I enter the house. 'Mum!'

There's still some light outside yet she's got the house as dark as a sex pest's dungeon.

'Mum?'

'In here,' she goes from the living room.

I burst in.

'I'm going to be the lead singer in a new band.'

'That's great,' Mum goes with all the enthusiasm of a used tampon.

'Did you hear me?'

'I heard.'

'I'm going to be in a band.'

'Sounds great, Maggie,' she goes without looking up.

Honestly, FFS.

'Dead dark in here. Want me to open the blinds?' I go, really wanting to yank them off the wall and javelin them at her face.

'No, leave them closed.'

Here I am delivering positive news, something that could be corner-turning, something to 'channel all my energies into' as Earth Mother Anna would say, and Mum's doing that adult thing that annoys the living crap out of me: she's yanking all the joy from it cos, obviously, my life's so insignificant compared to hers.

'It's a real band,' I go.

'So you've said.'

Stuff it! I'm opening those blinds, and I do. Pull the chord halfway. What's she going to do – throttle me for illuminating her life? Let's see how that one plays out with social workers and the NSPCC.

There's a rainbow in the sky; the final blast of the sun squints her face. You'd think she's in Ibiza or something the way she shields against it. No doubt she's been sitting on her arse all day, sucking nicotine into her lungs. Place looks worse than a piggery.

'What do you think about it then?' I go.

'It's fantastic.'

'We don't have a name yet, not a proper one anyway, but we will soon, then we'll start actual rehearsals and I guess we'll do some gigs. Then, after that, who knows.'

'I'm thrilled for you, Maggie,' she goes.

Thrilled?

Really?

Could've fooled me.

Man, it's as if I'd just told her I'm up the duff. With twins. Don't know who the dad is. Could be one of many.

Anyway, I'm sure she'll blow her mind when she sees us play. Might even crack a giggle.

'What's for dinner?' I go.

'Oh, I didn't have time to pick anything up.'

'I'll have a look.' I head to the kitchen.

Fridge: same, nothing exciting.

Freezer: some meat thing, fish fingers, skinny burgers, half a loaf.

Cupboard: pasta, beans, tomato ketchup.

I want chips.

'Mum!' I shout.

'What?' she shouts back.

'There's nothing here.'

'There's soup.'

'Don't want soup.'

'There's beans.'

'I want chips.'

'Look in the freezer.'

'Not frozen chips.'

'Well, have soup then.'

'Can I have two quid for the chippy?'

Nothing.

I can't see her but I know she's pure sighing. As if I'd just asked for a wrap of smack and a pair of Louboutins.

'Mum?'

Nothing.

'MUM?'

FFS.

I go into the living room again.

'Sake, Mum. I'm shouting.'

'Maggie, don't start.'

Don't start? Don't start what? I've steam billowing. Close to throwing a wobbly. And totally not my fault.

'I only asked for two quid to get some chips.'

'I've had a rough day.'

'What, sitting there?'

'No, I haven't been sitting here. I've been down the social all day, trying to get money out of them. I'm tired. I'm annoyed. So, just cut me a little slack, OK?'

'What did they say? Did they give you money?'

'They just told me what I was entitled to.'

'Which is?'

'Fifty-seven ninety a week.'

'That's it?'

'Plus twenty-seventy for you.'

'Seventy-seven-odd quid? That's all?'

'That's all,' she goes.

'Is that to pay the rent too?'

'Housing benefit will cover that.'

'You'll need to pack the fags in,' I go.

Her eyes snarl at me.

'I know what needs doing, Maggie, you don't have to remind me.'

'Just saying.'

'Well, don't!'

It's painful being in her company when she's a face on her like this.

'So, can I have two quid for the chippy then?' She frowns. I'm holding my anger in, trying to do that breathing-through-the-nose thing. 'I'm starving, Mum.'

She practically fires the coin at my head.

Should I put my hand on her shoulder to let her know I'm here, that I understand? Clearly I don't though.

'Thanks,' I go. 'You can share mine if you want.'

'I'm not hungry.'

I make my way to go, then turn; she's twirling a fag around her fingers.

'Mum?'

'What?'

'Did you check for jobs today?'

'Just go to the chippy, Maggie, will you?'

Comments

A good few weeks before the Moya thing, some rotten shit was plastered all over Instagram about her; could've been on more places as well, never heard. Basically, her cock of a boyfriend posted these pics of her. Nothing nude. Must've thought it was some big laugh though. One when she was mangled drunk and conked out on a floor, then another of her lying face down on a bed in her knickers. Wasn't the pics that was the problem it was all the comments underneath them, which obviously he didn't give a toss about, otherwise he'd have come out and defended her honour, wouldn't he? It was mad-vile stuff. Most of the names I didn't recognise, but there were some from school that I did:

Total dog!!!!!!!
Size of that arse, wouldn't piss on that.

OMG, did she even wash those knickers?

Is that an actual girl cos all I'm seeing is a steamin ugly skank?

Period pants!!!!!!!

Red neck if that's someone's burd

And that's not even a quarter of them. God, I was part sad, part mortos for her, and full-on useless.

I didn't phone to ask how she was, nor did I tell her I'd seen anything, cos a bit of me was hoping that she hadn't. Yeah, right, course she hadn't. We all know that teenagers and social media are like a cancer-injected rocket.

That night she sent a text: Im comin round

'Can you believe that?' she went.

'What a pure Weinstein,' I went. 'I hope you've dumped him, Moya.'

'Who?'

'That prick boyfriend of yours.'

'Why would I dump him?'

I was like, are we thinking about the same thing here?

'Cos of those Instagram pics,' I went.

'What Instagram pics?'

Oh, fuck, she actually hadn't seen anything.

'What pics, Mags? Show me.'

So, I showed her, and know what she said?

She went:

'He'd just bought a new phone and was trying the camera out.'

'Did he ask your permission?'

'Erm …'

'You're not even looking at the camera. And the state of you, you're a pure riot in that one.'

'I know,' she sniggered. 'I was buckled.'

'But look at the comments, Moya.'

She read.

Didn't bat an eyelid.

Didn't faze her; then I got annoyed at myself for getting annoyed on her behalf, especially when she didn't give a shit herself. If it'd been me in those pics I'd have wanted blood spilled. Why couldn't she see it?

I didn't go into it with her, wish I had.

Tears

It's not from the music, nothing in the tune's background. When I turn the volume down, the sound is still there. I put my ear to my door, listen. Short, panting bursts seep from Mum's room. Definitely crying. I picture her twisted on her bed, knowing that tears have arrived. Pure sobbing her heart out. I know the position. I know the emotion. I know I should go to her, but I can't. No way.

Heart

I turned the volume right down and played the music much softer. I lay there, ear to the mattress, waiting for the short, panting bursts to seep from my body. But I was definitely not crying. I was all twisted on the bed, thinking of what I could have done, trying to pure sob my heart out, but tears just didn't arrive. Still, these emotions caused my body to ache. Could I have done more for her, gone to her? No way.

Hugland

'Sit down, love,' she says when I come in from art school. Mum never calls me 'love'. This is serious. She's either won the lottery or it's something terminal.

'What ...'

'Sit down. We need to talk.'

'About what?' I go, chest chirping at me.

'You've probably noticed that I haven't been myself lately.'

You?

What about me?

What about me, Mum?

I don't even know who *myself* is any more ... What about ME, your daughter?

Remember her?

I'm here.

I exist too.

Truth: Mum's been an utter headcase since her dinner-lady duties stopped. Lost count of the times I've been like, 'Go have some me time for five minutes. But whatever's winding you up, can you please get off my case about dirty knickers on the floor or the state of the shower? Nobody cares. Put your brain back in.' And, get this, last week she was making powdered soup. I noticed her stirring and stirring for ages, not even looking at the pot; totally mongofied, pure glaring at the wall. That's not the best bit, oh no, cos I freaked out when I actually clocked what was happening: the gas wasn't lit. I was like, 'Mum, the gas isn't on.'

She just went, 'Oh, right,' ignited the flame and stirred her minging soup as if bugger all had happened. My face was like that stupid emoji with the wide eyes.

I sink into our springless sofa. Mum leans towards me, puts her mitt on top of mine. I'm totally positive it's something terminal. And all at once I feel like a spoilt-devil daughter. Her hands are moist. She smells like a showerless weekend.

'Mum?'

'I haven't been myself since losing my job,' she goes.

'Me neither,' I go, and instantly want to rocket vomit for making it all about my shit. Again.

'I know you haven't, Maggie. I know that, and I'm sorry I haven't been fully there for you.'

'You have,' I go.

She hasn't.

'No, I haven't.'

'Well, there's nothing anyone can do about it now, is there? We just have to get on with it.'

'That's sensible.'

'Tell me, Mum. Tell me what's going on.'

Her head falls to her chest.

'I feel really unhappy, really low.'

'Like bottomless-pit low?'

'Just feel a bit hemmed in, like everything's dark.'

Well, open the bloody blinds, woman!

'Are you able to see any light at all?' The lines in her forehead sink deeper.

She looks at me as if I've had a brain transplant. Like, is this my daughter speaking? It's a decent question. Truth: these are questions that Anna has put to me in the past. I banked them. Now, nicking them.

'I'm only trying to explain my behaviour, Maggie. I'm aware of what you're going through, so I don't want you worrying about me, that's all.'

Going through? Funny how we rarely mention the M word these days.

I take a quick gander at the living room. Place is a complete dive.

'I'm tired all the time,' she goes. 'But can't sleep during the night.'

'So, what do you do?'

'I sit.'

'In darkness?'

'Sometimes.'

My instinct is to say, 'What, like a mental patient?' but I restrain myself. I don't contort my face.

'What, just sitting doing nothing?' I go.

'Pretty much.'

'Is it cos you're worried about me?'

'I worry about lots of things.'

'Money?'

'That never leaves me.'

'Is that why you cry?'

'Partly, but my body tells me to cry. I can't stop it.'

'What are you going to do?'

Her hand clasps her mouth; she shakes her head. It rocks actually. I've an urge to hug her, which would be super weird. We don't exactly come from a long line of huggers.

'I'm not sure, Maggie. All I know is that I want to feel like my old self again.'

'Really?' I go, all sarky-chops.

Then she starts bawling.

Shit!

She needs me to step up, take action. Maybe I should hoover or dust. This isn't some randomer who needs me, it's my mum. Love is a verb, Maggie. Do something. Act. I slowly reach out and place my hands on her elbow. Mum responds with one of those grimace-smirks. Then she practically falls on to me, howling her heart out. I don't know where to look or what to do with my hands, so I wipe tears from her face and hold her like a baby. What else am I supposed to do? There's no manual on this, people.

Her cheap mascara stains my fingers and white T-shirt too. No soap powder alive will get this crap out. Good mind to storm straight into Primark, kicking and screaming: 'Here, you lot, your mascara is a total rip-off. It's not even sad proof. Money back now or this place is getting wrecked!'

After breaking our hug we sit in silence for a bit. Mum stares at the blank TV screen. My muscles are tense, wondering what she's thinking. I mull over what songs could be played at a funeral. Her belly goes up and down and I try to follow the rhythm, to be at one with her.

'Mum?'

'What?'

'I'm sad that you're sad. I don't want you to be.'

'It's going to be OK, Maggie. It's losing my job that's ...'

'How's the search going?'

'Disastrously,' she goes, looking much sadder. Some help I am.

'Don't worry, something will ...' I stop myself mid-flow cos thinking about her plonked here miserable all day scares the shit out of me. People do stupid things when they're skint and directionless, when they're so paralysed they can't think straight. The fucking stupid bastards do fucking stupid things cos they're fucking stupid bastards. She can't turn into stupid; I won't let her. I won't let it happen again.

A tear drips and falls on my tights. Moist. Looks like an exploded map of Scotland on my thigh. Bit of dust from the rank carpet must have shot into my eye.

Yeah, right.

Piss off, Moya, this isn't your time.

Oh, God, Mum's noticed my eyes.

'Come here,' she goes, and pure love assaults me again.

I gasp for air, my belly shudders; body moves with the tempo of hers. She puts her hands on the back of my head, squeezes her cheek into my neck. Think she wants to tell me everything's going to be fine and how she'll always be there for me. Shouldn't I be the one doing that?

She releases me. My head's throbbing. Raging cos I let Moya in again. I let her make it all about me and disregard Mum. It's a pressure cooker inside me. Heat rising. Something's building. I boot a glass that's sitting on the floor. Breaks into three tidy bits. No need to hoover.

'Maggie!'

I sense myself being angry with Mum. Probably thoughts of her watching soaps like a complete saddo night after night. Spending chunks of our food money on cheap wine and fags. Any wonder she's in a fug?

'Sorry for breaking that,' I go.

'It's fine – just clean it up.'

What a night, like a ride without a seat belt.

I manage to snaffle one of the shards of glass without Mum snaring me.

I feel that other stuff happening. It's a real slow-burner, sneaking up and kind of occupying my body. First comes the little voice in my head, then it's the tingling sensation. As if my skin's starving for me to do it, pure salivating for its dinner.

God, I so badly want to do it. It's a proper need.

I'm all nerves and excitement. Give me something. I'll use anything. Smashed bottle. Sharp tooth. Snapped chopstick. Crushed can. Any one of them could do a job on me. But what gets top billing is this shard of glass glistening in my hand. It's time. And I'm aware of how much of a fucking eejit I'm being. I am. It takes all my willpower to do it. Takes a superhuman effort not to.

Here's what I do:

I pull Larry, my cuddly toy, to my chest. Stroke my cheek against his. Kiss his tiny lamb nose. Lift his floppy ear and whisper:

Mum's completely losing the plot by the way.

Moya's like, *Could be that menopause, Mags.*

I'm like, *Menopause?*

You know, when they lose all the feeling in their fanny and stuff?

Think so?

I'd say so.

I'm like, *God, hope I don't get that.*

She's like, *We're women. It's a cert.*

Shit!

Do you not know anything, Mags?

I take Larry, my secret, and put him in that crucifix position like she did that time. His little marble eyes and threaded grin calm me. I lie beside him. Her. Shard of glass resting in my palm.

Mum might be feeling rubbish but I think I'm going completely fruit-loop. I plant my head on top of Larry's belly, laying it there for about fifteen minutes solid. I don't cry. I feel her hugging me back. Is that a tear on my cheek? SHIT STICK!

Maggie? Moya goes.

What? I go.

Remember that last film we watched at the cinema?

The dying girl one?

Yeah.

Was rubbish.

I know, but remember she made that list for herself?

The bucket list? I go.

Maybe your mum could do her own list.

She's not dying, Moya.

No, I know, but …

But what?

I feel it rising; someone's switched on my internal blood kettle. Moya knows the signs. Her face relaxes. Leans away.

Maybe there's something your mum's always wanted to do but hasn't had the opportunity. Something that would make her happy?

If I were a dog, my tail would be pointed skywards, gnashers on show, snarling. I pick Larry up, stare him/her out.

Like, what sort of things are you thinking? I go.

Well, she ...

What, get her nipples pierced?

Her eyes sparkle.

Something like that, she goes.

Think Mum's too old for the whole make-a-wish shit, Moya, don't you?

You're never too old to wish.

Maybe Moya's got a point. Maybe I could just ask Mum if there's anything she'd like to do in life; something that wouldn't cost money, which narrows it down a bit. What costs nothing? Sauntering around shop windows? People-watching in town? Yeah, make a wish, Mum.

I'm not asking my mum if she wants to pierce her nipples, OK?

OK.

So, get that image out of your head.

What image?

I mean it, Moya, don't even think about it or I'll kick the shit out of you.

OK, unthinked, she goes.

I hear her inhaling breath. *But ...*

Don't!

No, hear me out, Mags.

I'm waiting, I go.

She clears her throat.

71

Maybe she just needs to find someone.

What?

Like a man friend or … she goes.

I don't speak, mainly cos if I do it'll be a spew of swear words. And not the good ones either.

I let her dig deeper. *Maybe she needs to get herself a ride.*

From a boyfriend?

Oh, you're good.

So, you want me to find her a boyfriend? That what you're saying?

Is that so bad?

If Moya wasn't … you know … I'd swear she's been conspiring with Anna about the need to get my mum back on the man horse again. In more ways than one.

And where will I find this boyfriend, Moya?

You could look on …

Shall I check my arse to see if one's hiding up there?

It's just a thought, Mags, she goes.

Just a thought?

Yeah, that's all.

I fall back on the pillow.

Just a thought, I say over and over in my head.

Just a thought.

And I find myself thinking about it too.

One Minute

'Do you know what catharsis is, my lovely?' Anna goes.

As always when she uses her intellectual words I glare at her: *Speak English, woman, or I'm making a beeline for the exit.*

'No idea,' I go.

'Catharsis is like a purification of …'

'Honestly, Anna, if you don't start speaking the Queen's, I'm done for the day.'

'OK, let's put it another way, shall we?'

'No *we* about it. *You* put it another way.'

'You know what emotions are, Maggie?'

'Is that a question or a duh moment?'

'It's a rhetorical question …'

I shake my head and talk to the floor: 'What's with these whopping words?'

'All I'm saying is that the emotions we harness have to be released sometimes,' she goes.

'So we don't bottle them?' I go, deciding to play the game. 'I know this already.'

'I know you know it, but many of us have difficulties ridding ourselves of our negative emotions.'

I sit very still and very straight. No rocking. No hair flicking. Or pouting.

'There are techniques that we can use, Maggie.'

'Bet there are.'

'To help understand deep-rooted emotions.'

'Maybe I don't want to rid myself of them – ever thought of that?'

'I firmly believe that specific emotions need to be flushed out, my love.'

What is she, a healing plumber?

'And that will help me?' I go.

'I'd hazard a yes.'

'Oh, you'd hazard a yes, would you?'

'People tend to feel better after a good emotional flushing.'

'And that's the meaning of that word you said?'

'Catharsis?'

'That's the one.'

'Purging of the emotions. Letting them escape from your soul, body and mind.'

'Brilliant.'

I slump further into the chair as well as my sanity.

'It came from the Greek playwright—'

'Stop!' I go, putting my hand up. 'Useless info.'

'On the contrary, Maggie, talking is a terrific starting point.'

'Talking about what, anything?'

'Exactly.'

'Please!'

Anna draws in air, not like normal people would; she makes a massive deal about letting oxygen envelop her very being. Eyes closed. Looper.

'Dealing with a traumatic event is difficult enough for adults to contend with, Maggie.'

'Wouldn't know – not an adult, yet.'

'But with the developing adolescent –' she flat-palms her hand at me – 'it could be a real emotional hindrance.'

'I'm fine, Anna.'

'On the outside, my darling. The exterior. What I'm interested in are the goings-on in here.' Anna pounds her left boob.

'Blood and guts. That's what's in here,' I go, clobbering my own boob.

She stands up, extends her arms like she's about to hug the world, rummages through her bookcase, pulls out a piece of paper and hands it to me. I yank it begrudgingly cos I know what's coming.

'I want you to do something for me, sweetie.'

She seems to think that playing these textbook mind games makes her all cutting edge and relevant; that she's breaking new psycho-healing ground or something. Newsflash: she's not.

Example One: Brain Teaser

A man carries his son into the hospital because his son has been terribly injured. The surgeon walks in and says, 'Sorry, but I cannot operate on this boy … he is my son.' Explain why this happened, Maggie?
My answer: Who gives a shit? I'd let the boy die.

Example Two: Word Association

I say egg. You say, for example, omelette. I say sky. You say, for example, clouds. OK? Let's start. I … say … I say … Dracula.
My answer: Pure sex pest.

Secretly I enjoy Anna's games; it's a break from rummaging through my own grief.

She hands me a pen.

'What's this for?' I go.

'We're going to do a little experiment called spontaneous writing.'

'You mean, *I'm* going to be doing it?'

'That's right.'

'Magic.'

'Here's what's going to happen, sweetheart.'

'Crack on.'

'I am going to time you for one minute and all you have to do is write whatever comes into your head.'

'Like a story?'

'Don't think about it in terms of telling a narrative story, just write.'

'Like any old crap?'

'Just write.'

'Just write?'

'Don't worry about spelling and punctuation.'

'I'm not.'

'The exercise is simply to pop down anything that comes to mind.'

'Why?'

'It will all become apparent.'

I twiddle the pen between my fingers. Anna pulls her watch up to her face, all dramatic as if anyone cares.

'OK, my lovely. You have one minute starting from … starting from … now. Go.'

I gawk at her.

'Write,' she goes, egging me on as if I'm her daughter on the first day of school. 'Go, on.'

I put pen to paper.

This is as useful as tits on a fish. as if I didnt have enough on my plate without this analysing the state of my mind shit. Mums having problems. I might have to find her someone to love. will that help her? who knows. Still trying to deal with being me, and dealing with stuff. mums lonely. Im lonely. feel like Im orphaned from society. don't need any of this.

Pause

Pause

Pause

Thinking

Thinking

Thinking

Sometimes I smell you and I can't fuckin go on. Can't fuckin move. The sting is still fuckin raw. And you get to feel nothing. What the fuck do you feel? I want to know. I want you to tell me. I want to stop this ANNA.

I put the pen down.

'Finished, sweetie?'

'Yup.'

Anna cups her hands. I fold the paper up and place it into her paw.

'I don't know what that was, Anna,' I go.

'Oh, don't you worry yourself about this, Maggie, love. It's just for my files.'

'You're not going to read it?'

'Oh, I will. Once you've gone, I'll make some tea and have a read.'

Grief counselling? Money for old knickers if you ask me.

Rage

I'm late home. Been sitting in the library pretending to study. I know, me in a library – bonkers, isn't it? A girl's got to do what a girl's got to do.

Kitchen's full of cigarette clouds. She doesn't even bother her hole going to the door now. She's at the table. Legs crossed, facing out. Eyes on the invisible prize.

Nothing on to boil. Or fry. Or bake. Or toast. She doesn't say a word. Couldn't care less that she's a pure joy-stealer.

I literally walk in and walk out again.

Slam the door, hoping the noise will reset her brain to know I still exist.

Anger

I was early going to school. Said we'd start studying together (or pretend to) and arranged to meet in the school library. I know, us in a library – nuts, isn't it? Girls have to do what girls have to do.

Library was quiet that morning. Some nerds and the Muslim crowd. I sat at a table, waiting. Legs crossed, facing the door. Eyes on the prize.

Nothing in art. Or history. Or French. Or home economics. For three days she didn't appear. Couldn't care less that her exams were in four months.

Thought she could literally walk in, sit her exams and walk out again.

I knew some guy had something to do with it.

Always some guy. She didn't give a toss; that was Moya.

But this time I wanted to slam her head into a door and reset her brain.

Band

(Before notes plucked, chords strummed or lyrics belted)

I'm having a pissed-off-with-the-world day; zero desire to see any of them. Nor to be in some rank band. But here we all are, sitting in one of the art school's empty studio rooms. I'm no singer. I'm not one of these people. They're fresh-faced and wholesome; what am I even doing here?

I need this.

Oh, just shut up and get on with it, Mags.

Rap it, you.

'Me first,' Alfie goes, as if he's waiting to see Santa.

'Inventing band names,' Davis goes. 'I love this shit.'

Who says 'I love this shit' around here? Mean, does he live in Netflix? But, know what? I do like the way he says it.

'Erm, yeah, I love this shit too,' I go.

Who even am I?

What a lick arse you are, Maggie Yates.

'Let's hear what you've got, Alfie?' Plum goes.

'OK, ready?'

'Well, yes,' Plum says. 'We are.'

'Right, I think we should call ourselves the Headers.' Alfie grins and nods his dome as if he's just cured cancer.

'Like headers in football?' Davis goes.

'No, like headcases, nutters, mentalists,' Alfie goes. 'You know what I mean, Maggie, don't you?'

'No, why would I? Speak for yourself,' I go.

Davis laughs. I made him laugh. And with the flash of his teeth, a chemical thing happens within me.

'Don't get it,' Plum goes.

'Nothing to get,' Davis goes.

'I'm not sure I like it,' Plum adds.

'OK, vote.' I go. 'All in favour of the Headers, raise hands.'

No flaccid fingers point skywards, apart from Alfie's. He takes his boot to the balls with good grace.

Who cares what we're going to call ourselves? Not as if we're going to be Oasis. *The*-something bollocks has drifted far from my mind. Who can I blame? Probably Mum, yeah; all that woe-is-me guff is doing my nut in.

Davis has a 'belter of a band name', keeps asking if I want a clue. Totally flirting with me.

I'm in the humour for nothing. My stomach's acting like

it's been minced; the skin on my legs stings whenever they rub together. Why did I walk? Walking is good for clearing the headwebs, isn't it? A bit of Maggie time. Basically, I feel like shit and look even worse. No way could Davis ever fancy this.

Davis, all eager-beaver, sits rigid on his chair; I'm intrigued to see what brilliance will ooze from his mind.

'I think we should call ourselves the Damp,' he goes.

'The Damp?' I go.

'The Damp?' Alfie says.

'The Damp,' Plum whispers to herself.

'The Damp,' Davis goes again.

'The Damp?' I go again.

'Don't you get it?' he states, flashing me his eyes.

'Get what?' I go.

'Don't you guys get it?' he says to Alfie and Plum.

They don't.

No one *gets* it.

'Well,' he goes, 'the Damp is the initials of our names. D for Davis, A for Alfie, M for Maggie and P for—'

'Yeah, Davis,' I go. 'It's an acronym. We get it.'

'Oh, I really like acronyms,' Plum adds.

Jesus, Plum lives on the edge. She'd better watch out in case this love of acronyms leads to a love of crack.

'An acronym! Totally like that,' Alfie blurts, clearly no idea what an acronym is.

'What do you think, Maggie?' Davis asks.

'I don't love it, but I don't hate it either,' I go, which is true.

'OK, show of hands for the Damp?' Alfie belts.

Davis's and Alfie's hands shoot up, stiff as death. I follow, but mine is crooked at the elbow so it's more half-hearted. 'Giving it a maybe. See what the options are before committing myself,' I go.

'What've you got, Plum?' Davis goes.

'The Flaps,' she rips out without pause or hesitation.

WHAT?

THE FLAPS?

Wait, Miss Prim Pants didn't just say that, did she? NO EFFING WAY!

I snort.

'The what?' I go, for verification.

'The Flaps,' she rips again.

Verified.

I want to wrap my arms around her.

'Love it – you're hilarious, Plum,' I go.

There's only one other person I've called hilarious. She'd be disgusted at me, I know she would. Betrayal pangs dim the glow in my face. Now's not the time for M-word thoughts, Maggie.

Davis and Alfie snigger behind their hands.

'That not a bit rude, Plum?' Davis asks.

'Bet your arse it's rude,' Alfie goes.

'Come on, we can't call ourselves the Flaps,' Davis adds.

'My mum'll kill me if I'm drumming in the Flaps,' Alfie states.

'Well, I really like it – way to go, Plum,' I go, holding out my hand for that high five. Plum spreads hers out, gives me a tiny wave instead.

Pangs still remain.

'But, Maggie,' Davis says. 'While it can mean the flaps of a tent, it also means the …'

'Yeah, I'm aware what it also means, Davis,' I go. 'It's inspired.'

'But we're not a girl band,' Alfie pipes in.

'So,' I go.

'So, we can't call our band after …' Davis points to my crotch. 'After … that.' I could've straddled him. Just for a kiss – nothing sinister.

'Far too weird,' Alfie goes.

'OK, hands in the air for the Flaps,' I go.

Two girl hands in the air.

I joke-snarl at the lads.

They look at the floor.

'Sorry, Plum, I tried,' I go.

'I didn't think they'd go for it anyway,' she says.

'When we decide to dump these two losers, we can call ourselves the Flaps, deal?' I go.

'Deal,' Plum goes.

'What've you got, Maggie?' Alfie asks.

My turn to look at the floor.

Pure rotten being all-mouth-and-no-action girl. That's just me, I guess. I lightly tap my thighs. Then it comes to me.

'The Scars,' I blast out.

Silence.

'The Scars?' Davis goes, face knotted.

'We can't call ourselves the Scars. People'll think we're mental,' Alfie snorts. 'They'll slaughter us when they realise we're just four completely normal people.'

Normal?

Oh, if he only knew the half of it, or saw my thighs. Don't think normal lives in my brain.

'People'll laugh at us if we're crap not cos of our name,' Davis goes.

'Not after we practise and get shit hot they won't,' Alfie goes.

'What do you think, Plum?' I go, hoping for some female backup.

'It sounds pretty aggressive to me, Maggie,' says the Flaps girl.

'OK, hands in the air for the Scars,' Davis goes.

Dead space.

I don't even vote for myself.

'You're such squares,' I go.

I take *my* boot in the balls with poor grace.

And so, we're officially branded.

Welcome on stage … the Damp!

*

I position myself in front of the mic. The others warm up by plucking, twanging and sounding their instruments. I want to be sick. Mortos. Feel like I'm walking naked around town. OK, I'm ready.

Alfie beats us in. Plum follows. Davis hits the strings. I lean into the mic.

First proper practice. We sound worse than shit. Davis hasn't exactly mastered the guitar. Anything other than A, D and G chords confuse the hell out of him. Alfie has about as much rhythm as dads at a wedding. My voice rasps like I'm undergoing root canal. FFS. Plum is the only genuine talent among us. A proper musical whizz; makes you sick. God knows why she's chosen to be in a band with those two. And me. I know she's not my type, but I do like the cut of her jib.

The Bank

Mum's practically exploded my phone with messages. Needs me to pick up some food before the place shuts. Heehaw in the cupboards. Fridge empty. She must be starving. Why can't she do it? It's not as if she's snowed under with work, is it? I know she's unemployed but that's no excuse for laziness. What am I, a pure skivvy?

You can't just waltz in off the street, doesn't work like that; Mum's made an appointment for me to make the collection. I say nothing to no one. Before we attempt 'one last song' I make some dodgy excuse about having stomach knots and bolt. Plum gets women, the lads don't. We agree to rehearse same time next week. I want to tell Davis to batter round to mine later to talk songs, creative direction and stuff, but I doubt I could take the humiliation of a lame excuse; rejection slap. Doubt Mum would roll out the welcome mat anyway.

Knots do actually twist in my stomach as I approach the place. I glance around to see if anyone recognises me. Check over my shoulder. Coast clear. Free school dinners are one thing, but this is red neck times fifty. God, if ever Mum needed a rich guy in her life, or even a guy with a wage, this was it.

You can't take a list with you and simply pick from the shelves; no automatic doors to let you in and out; no glum security guard following you as if he's James Bond. There are no aisles. No checkout. No cards. No money. No payments. Best thing about the food bank? It's free. Worst thing? Everything else.

At the hall of the gospel church I press the buzzer. Look around again. Door opens. I can't keep my head upright. Hate this bit.

'Can I help you?' some old dear with a blue rinse goes.

'I have an appointment,' I go.

'What's the name?'

'Maggie Yates. My mum phoned earlier.'

She checks. Green light. I'm in.

I do like the worn-out wooden floors. Would make a decent rehearsal space. But I'm not a singer now, I'm a shopper. An errand slave. A scrounger. I don't even get an opportunity to browse; they've already made the bags up. Would it be rude to rifle through them, saying, 'Don't like that, won't eat that, that stuff's vile, that'd make me vom, you can keep those'? Would that be too offensive? Probably.

Five bags. Mean, how the buggery am I going to carry five

bags home? Five bags with a ton of tins in them: beans, soup, rice pudding, tuna, ham, more soup and more beans. Dead heavy things like sugar, rice, jam and potatoes. Who needs a gym? Few trips home from the food bank and your muscles will never need a steroid again. Five bags of different sizes and companies; everyone will know where I've come from. Devastating for the street cred. But this is the new helpful, caring and mature daughter in me. I'll be all over that soup like a pig in a trough.

My hands are falling off me. I battle on. No rest. It's an endurance test; see how long I can deal with pain, similar to when I'm under the shower with the nozzle turned all the way to red. Steam everywhere.

My arms feel wobbly with the stress. I know I should stop, have a breather. Means I've lost though, doesn't it? I've let it defeat me. No chance that's happening. I'm a warrior. Xena without the tits and leather. I lumber on, sweat all over the place: back of my knees, puddle in my belly button, moist thighs. Teeth gritted with every step. Pre-art-school Maggie might've chucked the five bags all over the road. Moya would've been with me, urging me to do it. Pure army of tins rolling about and us trying to kick them off each other's shins. And we'd have sat pissing ourselves as the birds tried to suck up alphabet spaghetti. If only.

I practically crash through the front door, into my cheerless house. Council don't give a shit about light, or people like us. Mum's watching *Dinner Date*, which is looped on some dodgy channel. I hear it. I'm guessing she's watched six in a row.

'That you, Maggie?' she goes.

Who else would it be?

'Yeah,' I go.

Whatever you do, don't get up to help, just sit there on your cake hole.

'Get the stuff all right?'

'Yeah.'

Honestly, don't dare get up and help.

No, no, no, you sit where you are.

You OD on *Dinner Date*; don't mind me.

I'll unpack as soon as I oxygenate my lungs again and stretch the rawness out of my hands.

I'm pure raging, want to go full metal racket on her; do something. Anything. Can life be that bad? Mean, seriously, it's such a luxury being flaked out in front of the telly every day. Wish I could do it.

I drag the bags into the kitchen and start unpacking the loot.

'What did they give us?' she shouts.

'Soup,' I shout.

'What kind?'

I rummage.

'Tomato … lentil … chicken … another chicken.'

'That's decent,' she shouts.

'Want some chicken?' I shout.

'No.'

FFS, no joke.

Larry

Right, that's it, I've had my last Pot Noodle in here while Mum watches mind-numbing TV. Don't want to be a total heartless bitch, but it's nicer spending time on my own. It's not that I don't give a hoot about Mum getting laid off; I do. Who wants to be worse than poor? I just don't know how to be around her; can't keep nipping her head about jobs or asking if she managed to get out of her chair today, can I?

I take the food to my room. Open Instagram. God, I hate Instagram. Close it. Do the same with Twitter and Snapchat. I should be with her.

It's time to find her a man: some trouser who'll make her feel wanted and vital. Some sad cardigan who likes nothing better than sofa nights watching people on talk shows who think they're important. Some boot-cut who'll part the clouds for her. Who knows what the power of a man charmer will do: keep her afloat? Be a human life jacket?

Maybe I should get one for myself; Davis is definitely on the list. Oh, I see him put on his best personality when he's around me, trying his hardest not to be a dick. To ooze cool and appeal. Or is that just me who's doing that?

If he thinks I'm easy, he's pissing in a typhoon. If he snares me – or whatever – then he'll be keeping it well tucked away. Be assured.

It was Anna's idea that I keep a diary. Course it was Anna's idea; who else would suggest such life-coaching guff? She wants me to fire all my thoughts and feelings into words: *charting the progressions and regressions* kind of compost. Even gave me a flowery notebook to kick it off; much better than social media purging. You won't catch me fishing for comments or hoping to get triple figures in likes or RTs.

Disclosure, I did try the whole diary thing out, mainly cos I'm a numpty. I was rubbish, all I did was drew pictures of 'the Maggie Yates Autumn Range' and commented on the clothes that Alexa Chung, Beyoncé and Lady Gaga pranced around in.

After designing a maxi dress fat people won't look ridiculous in, I scribble the heading:

Finding Mum a Fella

Then a subheading:

Maggie's Six-Point List: (the dream)

1. Must be easy on the eye. (Needs to be someone who gets housewives foaming: a George Clooney or Gerard Butler.)
2. Must be loaded/well off. (Shirt and tie gear has to be worn to work with a monthly wage coming into a bank account.)
3. Must own his own house. (Not some flat above a kebab shop – this has to be a proper front-door-back-door gaff.)
4. Must be childless. (There's no place in this situation for a pain-in-the-arse twiglet.)
5. Must be healthy. (Not freaky though, like drinking his own piss for breakfast or anything like that.)
6. Must be liked by me.

Larry's perched on my bed, the little slothy lamb that he is. Old enough to be my age. Old enough to be my best friend. I gaze at him. He tries to return my stare, but it's Moya's eyes that reflect back: clear, energetic and present.

I need her to check this list out; want to see her head shake, her cheeks balloon, her tongue rip the piss.

No way, Mags. You're off your nut if you think you'll find someone like that.

What?

Dream on, headbanger!

Girl's got to dream though.

But, Moya, there must be some …

You're surfing a rainbow, she goes.

Why? I go.

Cos guys like that don't exist.

Some do.

In la-la land, maybe. Not round here.

Got to aim high.

There's aiming high – she nods to the list *– then there's this.*

It's called 'blue-sky thinking', Moya, I go, doing that two-finger thing. Hate when people do that.

Blue-arse thinking if you ask me.

Her laughter sheets its arms around me; my body radiates as if it's been Tasered.

It's good to dream, I go.

Agree, girl, but the guys who'd make this list – she points to my pages *– are either married or living in films.*

You think?

I'd bet your virginity on it.

Well, it's no harm to see what's out there, is it?

I'll tell you something for nothing, Mags.

What's that?

Erm, HELLO! Wake up, smell the shit: male dreamboats don't live around here.

Just thinking what Mum would like, Moya.

But, you've got another problem, haven't you?

Which is?

Your big chick is only ever attracted to dickheads, isn't she?

True, I go. *Dickheads, deadbeats, tools, wankers. You name it. That's why drastic action is required. Especially now.*

Agree, Mags, but that bar needs lowering.

Our eyes don't shift from each other's; Larry looks drunk the way he's flopped on my bed. Needs a scrub too. White wool gone grey; a bit rank. Yet, it's her voice that bleeds through me, so lucid. Can't believe this is happening again, thought the other day was a one-off. Thing is, it doesn't feel as bonkers as I know it should. Moya had a soft spot for Larry too, even though she used him to point out my non-existent sexploits.

No, you're dead right, Moya, I go.

Yeah, I know I am.

She gives me one of those trashy American *you-go-girl* finger swipes; can't explain how much this gesture makes me want to commit mass murder, a flapping red rag to the king bull. Moya always liked being right.

I bite my tongue. Literally. Dead sore; makes water piss from my eyes. I set about making a second list, writing in a fever. When I'm done, she goes, *Cross the palm,* and extends her hand to me. No joke, she does.

Larry doesn't flinch.

Maggie's Six-Point Realistic List

1. Must have both eyes pointing in the same direction. (At least a 5/10 on the good-looking scale.)
2. Must not be a scrounger. (Won't be constantly skint at the end of each month.)
3. Must have some sort of transport. (Doesn't matter if it's a clapped-out banger, just as long as he's not hoofing everywhere on foot like a freak.)

4. Must not live at home with his mum. (We don't want him moving in with us after six hours.)

5. Must not be a diabetes wannabe. (A pot belly's OK, but not some massive killer gut hanging over trackie bottoms. Or a takeaway obsessive. No slob for this job!)

6. Must have my seal of approval and abide by two rules: 1. Don't enter my space. 2. Don't try to be cool talking about bands and films and fashion. Things you know NOTHING ABOUT.)

This is more like it, Mags, Moya goes. I can almost see her waving the list in the air. *This we can work with.*

Glad you approve, I go.

How we gonna do it? Can't just pounce on randomers in the street and ask them if they fit the bill. That won't work.

Oh, really? Duh alert!

Unless you guarantee they'd get their hole.

Fuck's sake, Moya.

From your mum, I mean. Not you.

Yeah, know what you meant. Still!

But it's true.

How's it true?

That's what old people do, isn't it?

What?

Watch a bit of telly, drink wine, then go for a ride. She has that smug look on her face; know it well. *It's all they've got, Mags.*

Mum won't be drinking too much wine, I go. *Doesn't mix well with the purse strings.*

She'll still be watching telly though, and lack of cash won't affect her ability to ride …

Mum won't be riding anyone, got it?

Sake, Mags, chill the pill out.

I'm not doing this so Mum can get her hole, Moya.

I know, but …

But nothing. She's not exactly feeling God's gift. Last thing she'd want is for some bellend clawing at her. That's not why I'm doing this. I just want her to enjoy someone's company without any thoughts of shagging, OK?

Larry's plastic peepers glint. I can't hear Moya any more. His head droops. I don't hear her answer.

Got it? I go, louder.

OK, she goes. Voice soft, but I make it out.

Cos my mum needs a break, she needs some happiness; she needs to meet someone who isn't a complete dick. Not too much to ask, is it?

I'm trying to hold it together. I feel it floundering at the back of my throat. I clench my fists. Tense legs. Can't let Mum hear me. God, imagine she did. Imagine she just burst into my room and saw me shouting at Larry. She'd have me sectioned.

I count to ten; Anna swears by it. I don't actually count, just breathe heavily through my nose and circle my wrists. My voice lowers. *It's not much, Moya, is it?*

No, she goes. She can't look at me. *It's not much.*

Right then, I go, not knowing how to continue our confab. Or rant.

I scrunch my toes hard, nearly crack them. The pain shoots up my legs until it hits the mark. Mission accomplished! Reward and release at the same time.

For some reason, I want to swing Larry around my head and bounce him off every wall in my room. It's tragic looking at his permanent string smile.

I boot the bed's base. Bad move. Hope Mum doesn't hear the thud or my howls when the stinging sensation kicks in. *Dinner Date* is far too important.

Big toe on my left foot has its own heartbeat it's pulsating so much. Might've given myself a fungal infection. Black toenail. Misshaped. Looks like a conker. Not a perfectly smooth, oily one that you can't stop stroking. No, this is one of those sorry-arsed deformed ones that you'd rather crush with your heel. Sometimes I think my brain looks like a deformed conker, too.

Toe is sore as hell.

So, this is happening then? she goes.

Maybe.

Suppose I'll help then.

How? I go.

She doesn't answer.

She doesn't answer cos she's full of shit; trying to push my buttons, tease me. Reminding me of what I'm missing. Anyway, she can ram it. I don't always need her.

There are ways, Mags, she goes. *There's always a way.*

Believe

She sat on my bed as I pure grilled her about missing school. Felt like a teacher. Told me she was hanging around with some guy most days.

'Doing what?' I went.

'Just stuff.'

Told me she thought school was for twats and sad losers. She looked like she was going to start bawling.

Told me how someone sent her some WhatsApp pics of a guy she fancied snogging some girl.

Told me she was fed up with people laughing at her all the time and all those online comments.

'They're just jealous, Mags, cos they're living life through a phone while I'm out there having a pure riot. So what if I like shagging – no crime, is it?'

'No.'

'What, girls can't enjoy sex too?'

'No.'

'Makes us cheap? Makes us inferior?'

'No.'

'Exactly. Don't think so.'

I tried to look surprised, as if I hadn't heard or read anything.

'Mean, everyone's got miserable fucking lives, Mags,' she went.

'Don't believe any of them,' I went.

Told me she absolutely didn't believe … I believed her.

Grilling

She sits on my bed as if she's about to pure grill me about something. Feels weird. Tells me she's heart-sorry for being the way she is.

'Why?' I go.

'Because I am sorry.'

'There's no need.'

'I'm going to try harder.'

Tells me she's happy to see me studying and enjoying school.

Hope she's not going to start bawling.

She pauses, her eyes droop, asks me if there's anything I want to talk about. Anything she can help me with. God, does she know I'm hurting myself? I try to look surprised.

'No, I'm good. Just the same stuff, you know?' I go.

'I know,' Mum goes.

Tells me she totally believes me … I don't believe her.

Singletons

Sign in the art school's computer lab says, *Desktops Are for Study Purposes Only*, but I spit in the face of authority. Should be researching fabrics and textiles; no brain for it today.

I type 'women seeking men' into Google instead. May as well have typed 'king-size cocks' as, even with a robust internet firewall, I'm bombarded with a smorgasbord of porn. I put in 'soul mates'. First few pages are of old people laughing on a beach. Too many pastel colours on show. Then it's back to more filth. I'm tempted to look, I am, but I'd probably get booted out of art school. God, why is the internet overflowing with saps looking for a hole to fill?

'Fruity,' the voice goes.

Oh, sweet mother of Lord! It's him. Davis. Pure standing behind me, staring at the screen. A woman in bondage gear has popped up.

'Davis!'

'She a relative?' he goes, nodding to the screen.

'No, no, no. I wasn't looking at that – I was researching …'

'That what you call it?'

'Honestly, I was.'

'Maybe you can wear that get-up in the band.'

'Shut up, you dick, I was researching for our project.'

I just called him a dick. That's me bombed out before the fuse is even lit. I'm such a tit, totally mortos. Is my face swelling up?

'Textiles project?'

'And fabrics,' I go.

He sits, wheels his chair next to me.

'Maggie, you can't kid a kidder, but it's completely fine with me – I'm the most non-judgemental person you could ever meet.'

'Davis, I was only …'

He holds his hands up.

'You should see the stuff that maniac Alfie looks at and I'm still his mate. Plum would have a fit if she knew.'

God, I want to kiss him, and not just a crap peck either. I've a craving to jump his bones, fully clothed though.

'Look,' I go. 'If you must know, I was trying to set my mum up on a date.'

His expression changes, eyes widen; such a vibe about this guy.

'You're not kidding, are you?'

'Long story.'

'Try me.'

So I tell him. Explain the issue, without the bits about our house being a pure piggery at the moment and our cash-flow woes in case he thinks we're a shower of tinkers. I don't say anything about the telly melting Mum's head. I don't go near the M word. Although if it wasn't for her I wouldn't be sitting here imagining licking this guy's face and struggling to help Mum out.

'We should look at the *Advertiser*,' he goes.

'The paper?'

'Yeah, their Hearts and Minds thing. Don't think they have bullshitters or pervs there.'

Wait!

Wait!

Did he just say *we*? As in WE? As in him and me? Us? Like doing something together, like a couple? Think my spleen is about to rupture. My mouth is dry. I wet my lips. NO, MAGGIE, do not lick your bloody lips in front of him.

'No, definitely no bullshitters,' I go.

'Right, let's have a gander then.'

I close the bondage lady and wheel myself to the side. Davis wheels into my place and starts tapping.

Belter of an idea. Belter of a guy.

Is every man in this country a sad singleton?

Artistic man, 43, not petite, loves rainy walks on the beach, poetry, unusual seashells and interesting rice dishes, seeks mystic dreamer for companionship, back rubs and more as we bounce along these tumbling clouds on life's beautiful, crazy journey. Strong stomach essential. Box No. 0990

Don't even have a beach within walking distance so I don't know what this tool's been smoking. And all that stuff about seashells, poetry and mystic dreaming? What a tosspot. No wonder he's single. For 'not petite' read 'requires two seats on a plane'.

Verdict: Rather Mum became a nun.

Bitter, disillusioned Glasgow man, lately rejected by long-time fiancée, seeks decent, honest, reliable woman, if such a thing still exists in this cruel world of hatchet-faced bitches. Send details to Box No. 0901

Send details?

Hatchet-faced bitches? You're lucky you're not getting a nail bomb in the post.

Verdict: I'd rather Mum got her bits sewn up!

Ripped hunk, washboard stomach, blond, blue-eyed, not-quite 45, WLTM woman with open mind and some experience of taking hallucinogens. Drop me a line at Box No. 0908

I can just hear Moya's voice: *I might give him a shout myself.* She'd be laughing, but serious though. You'd need eyes in the back of your head, honestly you would.

Verdict: Not on your goddamn nelly.

Employed in education? Me too. Stay the hell away. Man on the inside seeks woman on the outside who likes milling around hospitals guessing the illnesses of outpatients. 35–45. Glasgow. Box No. 0904

Sounds like a mad weirdo. We like him, even though we suspect he's a teacher. Lots of boxes ticked. I have a notion that he'd be a good fit for Mum. Davis agrees. Someone with a GSOH is the happy pill she needs.

Verdict: Strong possibility.

It's decided: we'll contact GSOH ASAP. Just write some drivel and send it off to Box No. 0904.

'You going to tell your mum first?' Davis goes.

'You mental? No chance.'

'That not defeating the whatever?'

'Think about it, Davis – what would you say if your child told you they'd been all over the internet looking to find you a woman?'

'Solitary confinement and sew their eyes shut.'

'Exactly – there's your reason then.'

Davis delves deep; thoughts flicker on his face. Looks uber clever when he's thinking, so cute. I stare at him, do my own thinking … of nothing in particular, just about my best mate.

What would you do, Moya, if your daughter presented this total-hot guy who wanted to date you?

How hot we talking?

Roasting.

I'd probably send him home with a limp, if you know what I mean?

Sometimes that girl needed a ladder to get her mind out of the gutter.

You wouldn't turn your nose up at the idea?

Correct and then some.

'Obviously, I'll make sure he's not on the rape register before I do anything,' I go.

'So, what are you going to do?'

'Set up a meeting.'

'Where?'

'Some duff coffee shop, but it'll just be me who turns up.'

'Cloak-and-dagger stuff. Like it, Maggie.'

'Then, if he measures up, I'll send him a sob-story email, saying how Mum couldn't make it and all that garbage.'

'Then set up another meeting?'

'Bingo!'

'*Then* tell your mum about that second meeting?'

'B-I-N-G-O.' I finger-shoot Davis five times in the head, then instantly regret it. Definitely thinks I'm a child.

'What if she doesn't buy it?'

'She will.'

'But what if …'

'God sake, she'll go for it. Trust me, Davis, I know my mum.'

'Only asking,' he goes.

I am such a rotten bitch at times.

'We'd better respond to this.'

I rip a bit of paper out of my notebook. Crack open a biro. Blue.

'Right, what shall I write first?' I go.

'One thing, Maggie.'

'What?'

'You shouldn't go alone.'

'Where?'

'To suss the guy out, you shouldn't go alone. So, I'll go with you.'

'You?'

Has this guy any idea how hot he is at this moment?

'Yeah,' he goes. 'Just to make sure ...'

'Make sure what?'

'Well, that you're safe, and ... er stuff.'

What is it with guys thinking all they need to do is twirl their manhood and we pure pander to them?

I'd pander with him anytime!

I wouldn't.

Maybe I would, actually. Oh, I don't know; I'm so confused.

'What do you think?' he goes.

'By safe, you mean that I don't get bundled into the back of a van?'

'You're way too terrifying for that to happen.'

'So why then?'

'Er ... cos I want to.'

'OK,' I go.

Foetal

Mum's entered grunting and skulking mode. Shifts from the kitchen window to the living-room window. Nothing happens. Nothing ever happens. Can't remember the last time I saw her crack open a book. I know reading's dead boring, but she always had one on the go. It's like living with this pure mumble-machine, too.

'Cup of tea, Mum?' I go.

'Huh?'

'Tea? Cup of, want?'

'Erm … erm …'

As if it's a major life decision.

Frustrating or what.

Sometimes I want to shoulder-shake her, yank her around by the hair. Last thing I saw her eat was a tin of rice pudding, about two days ago. I'm telling you, if you ever want to lose weight, just plunge yourself into a pit of misery. You might get a rash on your arse with all the sitting, but at least you'll be able to wiggle into a size eight.

'Can you pick up some milk and bread?'

'Now?' I go.

'Well, sometime today if you can. If you're not doing anything else.'

'Yeah, I'll pick them up for you,' I go. 'Just a few things to do first.'

I feel a FFS coming on. I don't. Change is hard.

'Thanks.' She scuttles off to whatever drivel the telly has to offer.

I bolt to my room.

I'm on my bed when Davis pings me a message to tell me how brilliant his guitar playing is. Big head. Actually, he is practising quite hard. At our last rehearsal I grunted my appreciation halfway through our cover of Feist's 'Graveyard', nodding positively when his fingers sprang into action. Quite turn-on-ish actually. I should probably tell him how great he is, but that's too easy. Keeps him on his toes. Keeps me on mine.

My mind glides off to a fictional world: Davis has his arms around me, like any considerate boyfriend would. He's not my boyfriend, but you get the drift. Mean, I'd hate him thinking I'm one of those high-maintenance selfie girls who struggle emotionally cos I'm not funny enough on Twitter. Not me I'm afraid.

I pull Larry to my face, dig my nails into him, picture

Davis pecking my forehead, whispering into my ear:

'Don't worry, hun, I'll look after you. I won't leave you.'

Not sure if he'd actually say these words, but tough shit, Davis, cos I've just made you say them.

Is that a tear on my cheek?

He stares at me. Puckers up. He's coming in. I purse my lips; I'm so ready. But it's her bloody mug that appears instead.

You're not thinking about your mum, are you, Mags? Moya goes.

I'm NOT thinking about you, Moya. It's not always about you.

OK, pop a downer.

If you must know, I'm thinking about this cool guy from art school. You don't know him. You'll never know him.

Bet he's some posh knob-polisher?

Go away, I'm busy.

I visualise him beside me, here on my bed; inhale his scent and thrust myself upon him. We have our kiss; intense and schmaltzy. But it's just kissing, nothing to get wet about.

After the lip sesh it gets uncomfortably surreal; he plays a shocking acoustic version of 'So Long, Marianne'. God, guys and their guitars! I'm on the bed, stranded on Awkward Island, having to accept this abomination with a pained grin on my face. Those high notes are not friendly to his voice.

'Brilliant, babe,' I lie.

'Taught myself it last week.'

He hops off the bed, goes over to the stereo and puts something on. A 'doing it' playlist no doubt. Thinks I've no idea what he's up to, but I'm so on to him. Obviously, we're not doing it, as in the full IT. A light rumble and that's all he's getting.

Allowing Davis to enter my thoughts stops all others from butchering me. But as hard as I try pulling him to the fore-front of my mind, it always comes back to Moya; an obstruction, a pure clam-jam nuisance.

Anyway, back to reality.

I change the music for real and allow 'How Soon Is Now?' to penetrate my world. Always gets me, that song. Maybe the Damp can cover it? I feel unique and spoilt when I listen to the Smiths, as if their tunes are written specifically for me. God, how can people stand listening to cack like Rihanna or Little Mix? I don't get it. All they do is gyrate their bits into camera and ask us to purchase it. The Smiths only ask us to lie back and listen.

THUD!

It comes when it gets to my favourite bit of the song.

Your brain knows the difference between a normal thud and a thud for help. SCREAM!

Slices through the song; never heard Mum sound like this. Shakes me to the core. I bounce up, dive downstairs.

Can't get the living-room door open. I push. Shove. It only shifts a bit.

'Mum! What's happened? Mum!' I shout through the door.

'Maggie.' She's crying.

I shoulder the door. Still not budging.

'The door's not opening, Mum!'

She sobs like a toddler struggling to get words out. I can't hear the telly.

SMASH!

She's thrown something against the wall, then a piercing screech. Her body falls; I hear it smack the deck.

'Mum! Open the door.'

'I can't ...'

'Mum, have you fallen? Have you slipped?' My voice box rattles. No joke, I start booting the door off its hinges. Three times I kick. Three times I leave only a footprint.

'Stop, Maggie. I'm up.'

'I can't open it,' I shout.

'The chair's in the way.'

'What chair?'

'I'm pulling it away now.'

I hear something being dragged; she grunts throughout.

'Mum!'

'Come in,' she goes, then starts to whine again.

I pause to think: *Please don't find anything bad; please don't let it be a blood bath; let it be OK.*

She's in the foetal, body shaking. It's cold. No blood. I want to pick her up, pull her towards me, rock her and tell her I'll never cause any problems again, that from this moment on I promise to be her best friend, a daughter she'll be proud of, and I'll stop slashing the shit out of myself.

She's lying there; I'm weak and incapable. Clueless.

This shit wasn't covered in the first-aid course I took at

school. So many holes in my knowledge; don't know if I should wrap her in my arms, smother myself around her body or haul her up to the couch. What do you do with a broken mother? I stand like a total spanner, staring at her humiliation, all contorted on the carpet. It's the full shebang: pained patches on her face, wet clumps of hair streaked across her mouth and woeful weeping. I hold mine in.

Her hand reaches out to me. Now I know what to do. Comes naturally. I lie down, feed my legs into the little V-shape she's made with hers. Perfect fit. I drape my arms around her and tighten my grip, hoping to suppress her shaking. I even peck her cheek. She's pure putty in my arms.

'Don't cry. It's OK,' I go.

Her tears taste of salty wine.

Minging.

What's going on? I'm wiping tears from her face; that's not science's plan. Who fucked up and reversed the charges on that one?

'Please don't cry, Mum.' I kiss her again.

'Sorry, Maggie. I didn't mean to.'

'Don't be sorry.'

'It just came over me.'

'The tears?'

'Everything,' she goes. 'Felt a surge of anger. I started crying and couldn't stop. I wanted to wreck it all.' She's calmer.

'Like the chair?'

'I tipped it over, it fell on to the door.'

'Why are you on the floor?'

'Needed to lie down somewhere.'

The couch was about two steps away and easier to flop on to. But who am I to ask stupid *why* questions? I get her to a position where she's bent double against the arm of the chair. God, I couldn't have loved her more. My heart's practically exploding for this woman. My heroine. Shit she's had to put up with in her life: me and my nonsense, a wanker father, a string of arsehole men – and all with little complaint. How can she be anything other than my heroine? Mean, look at me, I throw tantrum grenades if she dares to enter my bloody room. Come on! Time to grow, Maggie.

But what's going on in her head? Do we have similar conkers? Hope not, for her sake.

I sleeve-wipe her face; streaks of mascara stain my clothes, again. In the old days it would've been:

'I can never get that stuff out in the wash. Why don't you just use the wipes I bought for you? Jesus, Maggie!'

Then I'd have screamed something at her.

And she'd have screamed something at me.

Then I'd have screamed louder.

And she'd have stared harder.

Then I'd have chucked something, stormed to my room and plugged myself into my music.

No more shit, Maggie.

No.

More.

Shit.

'Want to go and sit on the back step?' I go. 'Have a fag, maybe?'

'I do actually.'

I help her. Even light her cigarette. There's another ten minutes shaved off her life! How good am I?

She leans her head on the door frame, gazes into the back garden.

'You should have a jumper in case you get cold,' I go.

No answer, just puffs death into her lungs, staring ahead. Pure rabbit eyes. I watch her for maybe twenty seconds without a hint of a blink from either of us. Her shoulders tense. I reach down and flick some ash off her arm.

'Thanks, darling,' she whispers. Mum never calls me darling. Don't know if I enjoy hearing it or not; makes me nervous.

'Why don't you sit with me for a bit, Maggie?' she goes.

God!

We aren't exactly your let's-smoke-at-the-back-step-like-we're-in-the-*Gilmore Girls* mother–daughter combo. Even back when I was curled up in my own foetal, the day after Moya, she let me get on with it, as if I were carrying some sort of virus. Can't blame her for not wanting to catch what I had.

I squeeze beside her on the step, get myself comfortable and swat stray smoke away from my face. She slides into me. I'm sure she feels my boobs pressing her. Mad weird. A few bodily adjustments sees her relaxed and snug. I try not to let the fags annoy me, but it's utter rank-attack. Takes some

117

amount of willpower to sit here with her. We don't speak. Just sit, her inhaling, me watching. I blow gently, just enough to push the smoke into the wind. Mum coughs, then stops. Stubs out her fag. I listen as her breathing becomes smooth and regular. Everything is calm. I think of that Smiths song 'Asleep'. I actually sing the first few lines into her ear. A Smiths lullaby. My lips press against her head and I hold them there for ages. We have a moment, we do. So what.

When there's nothing left to sing, I heave myself up from the step.

Back in my room, I've written a text. It's ready to go:

hey hun, mums terrible 2nite, feelin like shit. so am I. miss you. Wish u were here. Vom!

But I don't send it. Cos there's no one to send it to, is there? I don't think there's a network that would reach where she is.

My mind skips all over the place, sees her lying there: all those tears, those inner scars. Agony drenching her. She needs to pack in the fags; they're not helping. Her teeth are the colour of piss-stained knickers and her breath's like your granny's ashtray. Mean, what man is going to want a bit of that? She'd better watch out or she'll wake up one morning looking like a care home resident.

I'm thinking Elliott Smith's tune 'King's Crossing' is the best fit for this shebang. Press play, plug in and off you glide. Pain? What's pain? Pain is just weakness leaving my body. That's a good thing, right?

I wrap a clump around my index finger, maybe five times, then wrench it from side to side. No give. I twist more; tug slowly in order to prolong the agony. Still doesn't come out. The girl online did it easily. I copy the process, then think, *Fuck it, I'll just yank it as hard as I can, see what happens.* And that's what I do. Spiral. Tug. Yank. Out. Doddle. Like ripping Velcro strips apart.

I glare at the dark mound of hair in my hand and feel nothing. I finger-tip the patch where I heaved it from. Not totally gushing blood, but it's bloody enough. Stings a bit; reminds me of a tattoo sting. I close my eyes, put 'King's Crossing' on repeat mode.

Lose count of how many times it plays or how long I doze for, but when I open my eyes I know instinctively what I've done. Course I do; the tuft of hair is moist in my hand. My hairless scalp pulses and throbs. I don't feel guilty or stupid or any of that other crap; just wanted to know what Mum felt like when she lobbed that chair around our living room. When anger and pain collide. Different kettles of fish and all that, I know, but that's the shit that goes through my head sometimes. Anything to banish that foetal image of her.

Easier than I expected. It was sore, but not eye-watering. A good sore. That's the point, isn't it?

I can cover up my patch, make sure I choose a section no one (obviously I mean Davis) can see. I'm not a complete daft arse, you know.

Spontaneous

'And how are you doing, my princess?' Anna goes. Hands resting on her crotch.

Princess? Me? Has Anna ever seen pink sparkly threads hanging from these bones? I champion evil witches and wicked stepmothers. I ain't no princess.

'I'm fine, Anna. Plodding on.'

'You're a trooper, love. You really are.' She takes her hands off her thighs and plonks them on top of mine. As if some muggy hands could eradicate everything. She pure stares at me like some hopeless MILF in a nightclub. I don't blink. No way I'm losing this stare-off.

I win!

She lifts her hands from mine.

'And how are you fitting in with your new educational surroundings?'

Just speak like normal people speak for once, will you?

'It's good. I like it.'

'Going on to further education is a big step, a big upheaval for anyone, sweetie. You have to be careful you don't allow it to get on top of you.'

Is that not the whole point of college life? So things *can* get on top of you?

Wink! Wink!

'I'll be careful, Anna. Brownie's honour. Think I'll be all right.'

Seriously, why wouldn't I be?

'You know, with the progress we've made, our time here is almost complete, Maggie. The health board only gives us so many sessions.'

'Yeah, I know.' I try not to sound dead excited.

'However, I can apply for more time if you'd like?'

'Yeah, maybe,' I go, knowing there's no danger of me wanting more time.

Meetings with Anna are designed to stop me from regressing into blaming and shaming myself; learning to deal with grief in a positive way. Good luck with that one. Sometimes I want to snatch her by the scarf and beg her to varnish this conker brain of mine, hammer out its deformity. Anna says wanting to take on the world is a normal grief stage; if someone pays me a compliment I'll hack them with my tongue.

She might think these sessions have helped overcome my demons. They haven't even scratched the surface. Mean, if I took my clobber off she'd soon know what level of success we're talking about, or what a complete balls-up she's made. Sweetie.

'How's Mum?'

The question is like a twang in the gut. Forces me to sit back. I look away. Bite a dangling nail on my pinky. This is on the tip of my tongue:

'Oh, you know, Anna. Mum's A1. She's licking her despair off the carpet most nights and smoking her lungs black, while I've taken to cutting my limbs and ripping my own hair out for the craic, and, do you know what? I'm strangely enjoying it. But apart from that, Mum's on top of the world.'

'Same. Total pain,' I go.

'And what is her job status?' Anna fans her palms out in stop-motion. 'Oh, don't answer that. We're here to discuss you, not other things. You hold on to that answer. You hold on to your thoughts about your mum, unless you want to talk about them, that is?'

'I don't mind talking about Mum.'

'Well, just take your time, sweetie.'

'She has good and bad days.'

'I'd say she has. Being out of work is debilitating.'

'Yeah, well, that's life, isn't it?' I go.

'Such a terrible thing for anyone to experience.'

I'm on the verge of blabbing to Anna about Mum's tears and thousand-yard-stare stuff; moaning about having to be a skivvy, big-mouthing it all to her, but, actually, what I need is to eject myself from this conversation.

'I did another one of those writing exercises, Anna.' And there you have it. Ejected.

'The spontaneous writing exercise?'

'That's the one.'

'Oh, lovely.' She clasps her hands together. I'm like, *OK, OK, don't piss yourself, woman*. 'That's progress, Maggie. And how did you find it?'

'Honestly?'

'Honesty is why we're here, sweetie.'

'Completely useless.'

She looks at my hair. Not sure if she clocks any bareness. I pretend to restyle it a bit. Her eyes lose their flutter; her lips tense. She's definitely clocked it. Tilts her body towards me.

'Maggie?' she goes, pure serious.

'What?'

'Were you feeling stressed when you wrote it?'

'My whole life is stressful, Anna,' I go. 'It doesn't just creep up on me – I wake with it.'

Her eyes flash to my head again. As sure as this town is one big shithole she knows.

'So, are you going to show me this writing piece?' she goes.

I rummage through my bag, pull out my notebook.

'It's just crap ramblings,' I go.

'Oh, I'm sure it's deeper than that.'

She extends her hand.

'Honestly, it's pure garbage.'

'There's always good that can be extracted from these things.'

She's desperate to feast her eyes on it. This ... spontaneous writing. Spontaneous writing that took me ages to do, over two days. Spontaneous writing that's really lyrics for the Damp's first ever original song. This is me pouring it out. Miss Creative Energy. I show it cos I know she won't tell me it's a pile of piss. Who doesn't need an ego boost? At worst, she'll think I'm a total zoomer.

'You better not laugh, Anna,' I go, handing her my untitled song.

'You should know me better than that, honey.'

She skims.

She reads.

Her eyes widen, her head tilts and, at one stage, she gnaws at her bottom lip. Actually, I don't care if she hates it; totally down with that. What band wants old people liking their creative ramblings?

Anna rests the notebook on her knees, thumb-flicks her hair. Shuffles her eyes between me and the words.

'Well, what do you think?' I go.

'"Girl, I'm coming to join you ..."'

'NO! Don't read it out.'

'Oh, Maggie,' she goes. 'I really don't know what to say.'

'So don't say anything.'

And she doesn't.

Box

Davis's idea: fake email address.

My invention: donna.m77@eirmail.com.

While he's making actual study notes, I come up with the response to Box No. 0904.

Hi, inside man, this might be your lucky day! I like nothing more than a good old mill around hospitals as well. Best of all, I'm brilliant at guessing the illnesses of outpatients. 95% success rate to date. Maybe we could mill together and I could show you the ropes? Don't worry, I'm not employed in education any more. Phew! donna.m77@eirmail.co.uk

I hold the letter in my hand, examine and re-examine. Wonder if I'm doing the right thing by Mum. Her knickers will definitely explode when she finds out; she'll be seething. I hand it to Davis.

While he reads, I delve into my bag and see Larry's little mush mingling among my books and eight tampons. He's my other art school chum. No one will clock him, so who cares? Always feel better seeing him.

I visit her. Picture her. Smile at her.

Moya, you there?

I'm here, Mags.

For how long?

As long as you need me.

I miss you.

Stop that shit. Stop it now. Hear me?

OK, stopped.

Right, what is it? she goes.

Do you think that bit about milling around together sounds slutty?

Sounds as though she'd be up for a laugh.

My idea of slutty and Moya's were way different. Probably why I always thought she'd find herself up the duff years before me ... cos she was too busy being *up for a laugh* and then ... oops, someone's spud gun's gone off.

Mum hasn't exactly been up for much laughter these days, I tell her.

All the reason we have to get the chick back in the thick.

We?

She cared.

Mum always had a smile for Moya. She liked her, but thought she was trouble. And, God, trouble loved Moya. Not half. Total girl of firsts: fags, booze, sex, hash, hard booze, loads of sex, more fags. Made me look like a convent dweller. I'm wired differently, I suppose.

'Davis,' I go, after he's read it twice. 'I'm not sure about the "I could show you the ropes" bit. Mean, it's a belter of a euphemism, but do you think we should cut it?'

'It sounds great. If I was the guy receiving that I'd be chucking folk out of the way to email back.'

'You think?'

'He'd be bonkers not to reply.'

'OK, let's do it then,' I go. 'You post it.'

He leaves me to my studies and shoots out to the postbox. Box numbers. What are those anyway? Who uses them? Why didn't he just leave an email address like everyone else? Box numbers suggest weirdo beyond belief. Freaks and Dark Web pervs.

It's always the same: after doing something you're unsure about, like angry tweeting, sending an emotional WhatsApp message or posting a bloody letter under someone else's name – mean, who sends letters now anyway? – you instantly wish to rewind and take it all back. You want to pick that computer or phone up and smash it against the nearest wall. As Davis runs down the street, I wish I could claw the letter back, that I could somehow squeeze inside the postbox and shred it, chuck a burning flame in its mouth.

Saying that, Mum deserves some romcom in her life.

I should be thinking positives about playing Cupid's daughter, like how cool this guy's going to be, how he'll think Mum's a total babe, how he'll spoil the bejesus out of her. But no, not me. I'm thinking that I've just booked my mother into the Josef Fritzl Hotel for a wicked weekend of tickle and torture. Maggie Yates, the Einstein of crap ideas. And that numpty, Davis, isn't far behind. He's got a cute run though.

Coffee

First thing I do is get on the blower to Davis.

'Davis?'

'Yeah?'

'You need to get round here fast.'

'What's happened?'

'The box number guy only emailed, that's what. Here now, or else. I need help.'

'Or else what?' he goes, sort of laughing.

'Or else nothing, just get your arse round here.'

I click the phone off.

Actually, the first thing I do is turn to Larry, who's lying under the covers pretending to snooze.

He's replied, I go, tugging at his leg.

I throw him up in the air. *Moya!* I murmur.

What?

The guy replied.

What guy?

I throttle Larry, squish his neck in one hand. His eyes don't bulge.

OUCH! What the … ? Moya goes.

Mum's guy replied.

No fucking way, seriously?

Seriously.

Better not be a douche, she goes.

She's started sleeping beside me again. I know, utter red neck. Kind of glad Mum mooches from bedroom to bog to living room and back again; don't ever want her earwigging into our confabs.

Hi Donna (I presume it's Donna?),

Thanks for your letter. It made me laugh out loud. Honestly, it did. I'd be delighted for you to show me the ropes as we mill around some hospitals together! But before we do that, would you like to meet for a coffee sometime? Somewhere in town perhaps? Date, place and time I shall leave to your discretion and convenience. I'm flexible.

Speak soon (hopefully),

Ian

My heart's racing. First time Davis has been in my gaff, my room. God, I hope he doesn't think he's here to mattress-test. Hopefully Mum'll be hypnotised to *Judge Rinder* and won't even notice he's here.

130

We read the email about twenty times.

'What do you think?' I ask him.

'Don't know. What do you think?' he goes.

'Doesn't sound like he's a fridge full of heads or anything, does it?'

'Erm …' Davis reads the email again. 'No … he seems normal … maybe even funny. Doubt he's got kidnapping on his mind.'

'What about his name?' I go.

'Ian?'

'Lame as shit, isn't it?'

'Better than Sebastian or Trevor.'

'Screams boring to me.'

'It's not that bad, mean, I wouldn't call any of my kids Ian, but maybe your mum'll like it.'

'Yeah, maybe.'

Shit, that's when it really hits me: how am I going to tell her? I can see this question coming in waves, gnawing at my mind. Mum'll be OK about it, cock-a-hoop that I'm helping her back on the horse, won't she?

'Well?' he goes.

'Well what?'

'What are you going to say to this Ian dude?'

'Don't know. I can't think straight at the moment.' I circle my temples. 'Bet Moya would know,' I whisper, then realise I've said it out loud.

'Who's that?' Davis goes.

'Nobody. Nothing,' I go.

I put some Joan As Police Woman tunes on. Davis looks at me suspiciously. When the music kicks in he lies on my bed, thumb tapping his belly as if he's a human bass guitar. Can't believe he's actually on my bed. Should I lie beside him? I want to, I do. But can you imagine if he sees my legs or runs his claw along my bare torso? May as well go live on an island for humiliated women. Stuff it, maybe I should just jump him, surprise his arse. He wouldn't know what'd hit him. Actually, no, consent and all that. Maggie, do not sexually assault Davis.

His fingers shift to his chest, making a low-pitched hollow sound. His head is next to Larry's. I watch them beside each other, my two people.

Who's that shit you're listening to? Moya goes, nodding towards the speakers.

Moya's into painful music: Drake. Kings of Leon. George Ezra. Kill me now. I hated it when she wore band T-shirts, as if I were guilty of shit taste by association.

You've done a job on this Ian guy, Mags. He seems like a saucy one.

I'm so tingly cos Davis is here. He doesn't know what I'm hearing; wonder if he realises what I'm thinking.

You taking the piss? I go.

Just a tiny bit.

Well, don't! This is no time for piss-taking. My nerves are all over the shop here, Moya.

Not sure about the name Ian though, she goes.

Exactly what I said.

We do a girl-power agreement slap. (Obviously we don't!) I hate people who high five. What's happening to me? Seriously, what is happening?

Ians all sound like they stack shelves in Aldi, Moya goes. *Or they've got a fine collection of gimp masks.*

She comedy-puckers her lips.

I laugh.

Davis opens his eyes.

'What're you laughing at?' he asks.

'Nothing.'

'Tell me.'

'Nothing, just a joke I remembered.'

'Love jokes,' he goes, and sits up on the bed. 'I want to hear it – I want to laugh too.'

Mean, fuck's sake. Can a girl not even enjoy her own thoughts without having to be pure cross-examined? Talk about control.

He pokes me on my shoulder.

'Come on, tell me.'

Now I've got to come up with an on the spot joke. Cheers, Moya.

'Right,' I go. 'Guy walks into a butcher's and asks if they've any oxtails. Butcher goes, "Once upon a time there was this big ox …"'

There's a processing pause.

Then he laughs.

Laughs hard.

Lolls around the bed laughing. It isn't that funny. He tugs me on to him, laughing. We roll around, laughing. Squash Larry under our bodies. I could've kept rolling; could've soggy-kissed and felt him on my leg as we snogged and spun more. I could've gone much further, like *much* further. But when it comes down to it, I just don't want to. Not while there are three of us in the room. I rediscover reality and roll off him.

Anyway, who knows. He could be gay.

Laughing feels good. I make a mental note to do more of it around Mum.

'So, what are we going to do, Davis?' I go.

'Email him back.'

'What?'

'When and where to meet.'

'Do you know any coffee shops?'

'You could suggest a hotel,' he goes, smirking as if he's just invented the internet or something.

'Yeah, let's suggest meeting in a place where there's loads of beds above them. Magic idea. She's not a fucking escort service, Davis.'

The words 'escort service' make him snort. God, what are guys all about? He's so chilled about my brashness. I could literally call him a grotesque dickhead (which he's not) and he'd crack a smile. Shit, is this soul-mate territory?

No, Mags, it's not. It's just an eejit in your room. You're the one who needs to chill.

'Well, I don't know any cool coffee shops, do I?' he goes.

'There's a Starbucks next to H&M.'

'It'll be dead noisy.'

'And?' I go.

'Well, they might want to … chat … talk softly … I don't know – I've never been on a date.'

I look at him, scrunch up my face and semi-scowl. Secretly delighted to hear this news.

'Starbucks is perfect,' I go.

'It is?'

'Totally. We'll send this Ian guy there.'

'Right.'

'Means we have time to suss him out first, make sure he doesn't have gloves and rubber tubing on him. He won't suspect a thing. He'll think we're a couple of teenage losers.'

Davis squints his eyes.

'And?' I go, holding on to the 'A' sound much longer than needed.

'What?'

'Well, what if he's a complete munter?'

He widens his eyes. Puffs out his cheeks.

'Er …'

'There's no way I'm sending my mum on a date with some guy who's got a face like two cats fighting.'

His features morph into a huge grin.

'Agreed,' he goes.

'We'll also be able to tell if he's jailbait material, pure eyeballing all the teenyboppers. He'll be getting nowhere near my mum if that's the case.'

'Like it,' he goes.

'OK, let's do it then.'

He puts up a high-five hand, but, honestly, the moment's crying out for a celebratory hug followed by a cracking lip-smacker. What good's a high five to anyone?

Guys and their stupid hands!

Who

I need to concentrate on art school, let her discover her own path towards love. Stop interfering. But my desire to help is bubbling inside.

What's the point though?

Mean, think about it:

Who'll be interested?

Who'll want to be around her screwed nut these days?

Who'll want to be with someone who's pure skint?

Then the question:

Will he only be after a quick shag?

People might see her with a new man and laugh behind her back. As if she's undeserving of happiness.

Graffiti

I don't know why I was raging when she came back to school; it was bubbling inside me. Not for her; it was all directed at him.

'What, you actually made it?' I went.

'Shut it.'

'You need to screw the nut.'

'Oh, there's tons of screwing being done, don't you worry about that,' she winked.

People laughed behind her back.

I was pissing one time and it's on the door.

Her name followed by: is a spunk vessel

Her name followed by: would shag yer granda (and granny)

I had to clean it with spit and toilet paper.

She's completely undeserving of this.

Book

I don't order coffee cos it's rancid. Simple as that. And the cups are king size. Imagine drinking out of those things. Massive bucket of latte. The world will be queuing up for a gastric band if they keep guzzling that stuff. They should just tie a huge one around the width of Scotland and be done with it.

I get sparkling water. Davis gets a tomato soup, in a cup. His death-row meal apparently.

Moya wouldn't be happy about Davis stealing her thunder, she'd be like, *Sake, Mags, you're not pure joined at the hip – he's got to give you some breathing space, know what I mean?*

I want us to have a feel of two people fully relaxed with each other, as if we've been on loads of dates before, unfazed by our bouts of silence, but I know that's pure pie in the sky.

Still, I'm glad he's here. I want him here. Not saying I desperately need him or anything like that, although it might be nice to need someone. Also, this Ian guy might be a brain cell short of being normal.

We're early; important to get a seat. Every minute or so we check our phones. Thumb the refresh button on the invented email.

We're supposed to be blending in, trying not to attract attention. Davis is twitchy. His soup's roasting. All the teens seem to be sponsored by Bershka or Hollister. Lots of backcombs and bare ankles on show to make me gag. Styleless clones. No individuality. No idea. I'd loathe Davis to have that look. And me. Mostly I hate living in this body, but times like this I'm glad it belongs to me.

We sit in silence, eyeballing everything around us. Listening to chiming china and drab chat. Gawping at the bored new mums on their eighteenth coffee of the day.

Lots of staring at the door. No sign of this Ian character. He isn't late. But anyone in their right mind knows it's a good idea to get to a first date early. Even though this isn't exactly a date. This is a meeting – nothing more than a quick 'Hiya, what's the craic? What do you do for a crust? What stuff floats your boat?'.

'I'm a bit nervous, Maggie,' Davis goes, stirring his soup beyond an inch of its flavour.

'Relax, or try to.'

'What if we don't recognise him?'

'We will,' I go.

'But how can you be so—'

'We'll know it's him as soon as he steps through that door,' I go. 'Look around.' He does. 'Do you see any old, single men in here?' He shakes his head. 'Exactly.'

'But what if …'

'Look, Davis, I'll know when it's him. He'll be shitting himself – it'll be written all over his mush. Guys have the same expression whenever they're out to impress.'

'We do?'

'See, thing is, men are always trying to be something they're not: friendly, intelligent, sensitive, not sex offenders, whatever. But everyone knows it's all a bullshit front – they're just terrified in case their façade drops or we see through it, which, let's be honest, in most cases that's a pure doddle. So, take my word for it, when this Ian geezer walks through that door, I'll know.'

I suck fizzy water into my mouth.

Davis jerks his head twice.

'And what am I then?' he goes, leaning back.

'You?'

'Yeah.'

'You're … er … you're … er … just Davis.'

Mean it as a compliment.

'Wow! You're good, Maggie.' He folds his arms. 'Pure doddle, eh?'

'Don't be a dick.' I flick water off my straw at him.

But he's far from being a dick. Would I be sitting with anyone that dickish? No danger. When Moya was going through her I-hate-all-men phase cos her latest monster in a tracksuit, or MOT as I liked to call them, couldn't keep his trackie bottoms hiked up, she saw nothing redeeming in the male world.

'He said he'd be reading a book,' I go.

Hi Donna,

Starbucks it is! Looking forward to it. Oh, so you know which one I am, I'll be wearing a rose in my lapel!!! Seriously though, I'll probably be reading a book (or pretending to).

See you,

Ian

What tool goes on a date with a book? Moya goes.

Tell me about it.

And what sap eats soup in a coffee shop?

He's not a sap, so park it!

'What numpty brings a book on a date?' Davis goes.

At least they agree on something.

'Let's stop calling it a date, Davis. It's not a date. It's a meeting.'

'Fine. A meeting then.'

'Actually, it's a nothing,' I go. 'Cos Mum isn't coming, is she?'

Davis sinks his tomato soup, licks the cup rim clean, table

manners of a knuckle-dragger. He plays imaginary guitar when he hasn't any conversation in his head. Thinks I'm blind, but I see his fingers subtly flicking and his mind coiling to remember chords and notes. Weird, but cute. Too cute. He'd definitely get it if I was giving it.

A girl at the next table fiddles with her bra cos she's wearing one of those small push-up ones that cut right in. Is tit elevation worth the hassle? Davis painfully fights the desire not to check her out.

Then I clock him.

He joins the queue. I know it's him straight away cos his face screams: shitting bricks. Job-interview mug.

I manage to get some major visuals of him from where I'm sitting. Face. Hair. Height. The full bhuna. God, he's the spit of that actor. Whatshisname? Can't put my finger on it. But, take it from me, he's the spit. Let's be clear about something: he's no catwalk model. But he hasn't been dunking for chips either. Result! Seven out of ten. Eight or nine with beer goggles on. Mum will approve.

Hundred per cent a teacher though. Clothes are a giveaway: duff half-trainer half-shoe numbers, boot-cut jeans with daft fake rips on the thighs, a starch collared shirt and a black cord box jacket. Sale at M&S maybe? Reeks of a rugby fan.

My eyes dart between the guy and Davis. My guess: Ian is an English or history teacher. One of those who wants to be everyone's buddy; the go-to teacher in times of baby-school crisis:

'Sir, we want a non-uniform day.'

'Sir, it's not fair that we can't have a Battle of the Bands event.'

'Sir, the sixth year should really have their own common room.'

The take-no-shit-in-class teacher who likes a bit of banter from time to time ... usually on their own terms. The low-self-esteem teacher who needs everyone to like them.

It's him. Defo. Can't be anyone else. The book seals the deal. *I shall probably be reading a book* my arse. You'll be alternating the thing between hand and underarm. Maybe it's his character flaw? Carrying a book about as if to say, 'Look at me, I read tons of books – aren't I dead clever?'

I don't mention seeing him to Davis at first cos I want this moment for myself. It's my game after all. I want to decide if he's worth further study. Mean, if I get a whiff of any wife-beater demeanour, we're hot-stepping it out of that door before you can say 'Want to listen to my *Thriller* album?'.

He collects a small cup of something and a sparkling water. Sits down, pulls his book from under his arm, cracks it open. When I spy the front cover my jaw almost scuds the table. YOU'VE GOT TO BE WRINGING MY KNICKERS! Who brings a book with *that* title to a first date? A meeting? What kind of special needs does that? Big yellow letters slap-bang for all to see: *A Man in Love*.

I wish she were here to back me up. To remind me that

I'm not going mental. Far too many of these where-is-she-when-I-need-her? moments.

What the fuck is that? Moya goes.

I know, right, I go.

'Davis, don't look,' I go, quietly. 'He's here.'

'You sure?' he goes.

'Yes.'

'Where?'

'Behind you. One o'clock.' Davis makes to turn his head. 'Don't look! Don't make it totally obvious. Move your chair so it's subtler.'

He shifts around.

Ian (the guy) is reading, or pretending to, and doesn't notice our movements.

'Guy with the book?' Davis goes.

'Has to be,' I go.

'He looks like that actor.'

'I know, right.'

'What's his name again?'

'Can't remember. It'll come to me.'

Davis squints towards him once more.

'He's all right, Maggie.'

'He'll do.'

He can do me.

Honest to God, Moya!

Apart from that book, doesn't seem like he owns a dungeon. I think your mum'll like him.

'Bit weird, that book,' Davis goes.

'A bit? Mean, if I were meeting some guy and they pulled that out, I'd run a mile.'

'Might be really good.'

That's not the point, boyf. Duh! Where did you find him?

Give him a chance – you'd like him, Moya.

I know what I'd give him.

Don't! Just … don't.

'The point isn't if it's any good, Davis,' I go.

If eyes could tut, mine would be tutting.

'So, what do we do now?'

'Let's leave it for five minutes then email him.'

'From here?'

'It'll save the poor sap sitting there all day waiting on nobody arriving.' I pick up my phone. 'What should I write?'

'Something like, "Sorry I can't make it cos I'm up to my eyes in work."'

My fingers begin to dance over the screen.

'I'll just ask if we can organise for another time,' I go.

'Think he'll want another meeting?'

'Look at him, Davis. He looks like a lost soul – course he will. He's a man in love, remember? Mum'll thank me for this in the future.'

The future.

I don't want to think about the future. Too much shit to consider. Suppose that's why we have that part of the brain where we can leave stuff languishing. A bit like left luggage.

146

I write:

Hi Ian,

Apologies that this is short notice, but I'm afraid I can't make our coffee meeting. Something last minute came up at work which I just can't get out of. I'm so sorry. I hope it won't be a major inconvenience to you. Could we arrange another time to meet? I'd really like that.

Speak soon,

Donna

No kisses, Mags?

Far too early for email kisses.

I show Davis.

'Yup, that's cool.'

'OK, will I send it?'

'Fire it off.'

I see no pages of *A Man in Love* being turned. Proving once and for all that he's pretending, that he *was* shitting boulders; faking it.

The book falls. He picks it up and places it on the table, cover side up; takes out his phone. The email has landed. He's reading. I inspect his expression. His face intensifies. Disappointment. He leans back in his chair, plonks his phone next to *A Man in Love*. Seriously disappointed. Lifts his book, opens it. Closes it. Flops it back down again. Majorly pissed off. Downs the rest of his drink. Game over.

Look at him, Mags, he's raging, Moya goes.

So would you be if you'd just been rubber-eared by a stranger.

'Don't think he's going to write back,' Davis goes. 'He's all fidgety.'

'Trust me, he'll write back.'

Ian (the guy) picks up the phone again; his fingers go like the clappers.

I refresh.

Puts the phone in his inside pocket when he's finished.

Refresh.

Shuffles his arse out of the seat.

Refresh.

Tucks *A Man in Love* under his armpit.

Refresh.

Ambles to the door.

Refresh.

Opens it.

Refresh.

Walks out of Starbucks.

Refresh.

Out of sight.

Refresh.

YES!

Hi Donna,

Work? I'm just glad you have a job and you don't need to bleed me dry! No worries, I fully understand. No inconvenience at all, just sitting here reading and drinking cold tea, but thanks for letting me know, otherwise I'd have had to have bought another one. Maybe we could say same time, same place next week, if that suits?

See you soon (hopefully),

Ian

I slink closer to Davis and read it to him, whisper it almost. God, he smells magnificent, for a student. For about three seconds my mind sinks into the sex sewer. No way he's getting me to do that.

'Sounds like a decent guy,' he goes. 'That whole thing about being glad she has a job is not like belly-laugh funny, but it's a good start. No?'

'Suppose,' I go, knowing full well he wouldn't be writing that shit if he saw her perched in front of the TV.

'You better write back to tell him next week's fine.'

'Now?' Davis nods. 'Will that not seem desperate though?'

'Shows you're serious and not a fannier abouter.'

'I'm not.'

'And ...'

'What?'

'You'll have to tell your mum; sort of important really.'

Honestly, it might just be easier to punch him ... which could then lead into a kiss.

'Right, shut up and let me think,' I go.

He pulls an imaginary zip across his mouth.

In the silence I write:

149

Hi Ian,

Can we say in two weeks? That would work better for me, if it's OK with you? Hopefully work won't be as crazy. I promise it won't. See you then? Same place? Same time?

Looking forward to it, and sorry once again.

Donna

You know what this means, don't you, Mags?

What?

You'll have to tell your mum now.

God, not you as well.

Even if *A Man in Love* isn't a long-term Prince Charming, I think just having this might give Mum the confidence to go out, meet some pals and talk about how shit their lives are. She'll have the sparkle back in her eyes. That's my thinking anyway. Still, I'm dreading telling her; tend to dread most things these days. I know a man, any man, isn't the cure to loneliness or unemployment, but it's a start. This is just me putting batteries into the toy, pressing *on* and hoping that the bloody thing works.

I'm in my own zone. A daze. I know I'm going to hurt myself tonight. It's a no-brainer. Not the hair again; too risky, too noticeable. Makes the blonde go red. Who wants to be a blonde redhead? And, anyway, I want to keep some of the things I think Davis likes about me intact. Don't know my weapon of choice yet, all I know is that it's happening. Dead cert.

When I play out the scene I despise myself – not cos I actually despise myself – cos I feel excited. But I guess despising yourself is all part of it too, isn't it? I can't control these thoughts. I've already rocketed over the line and made a pact with the demon inside and – know what? – it's invigorating. How did I get to this stage?

'How are you going to do it?' Davis goes.

'Do what?' I go, thinking for a nano-sec that he knows. He sees my thoughts projected above my head. My heart rains punches down inside me. 'Do what?'

'Tell your mum.'

'No clue.'

'Best to come right out with it.'

'It's giving me a pure migraine just thinking about it, Davis.'

'What's the worst that can happen?'

'She says no, disowns me and chucks me out.'

'Not going to happen.'

'You think?'

'Well, if she does, you can come stay with me.'

I don't have the heart to tell him I'd rather rough it. Wait, that's so untrue. I'd love to stay with him. Sprawled naked on his bed, listening to tunes all day, taking lengthy conversation breaks before going at it again, and again. I'll need an all-day playlist.

'I'll tell her this week or the start of next,' I go.

'Good idea.'

You're some daughter, Mags.

Trying to be.

Try to love yourself a bit more though, eh?

This, from you?

Wish I could remember the name of that actor so I could google him.

Meeting

She introduced us after school one day. He came to meet her at the gates, probably to make sure that was where she'd been. I instantly hated him. Strutting, head to toe in some cheap trackie, his skag uniform. I just didn't get it; wasn't as though he was God's gift or anything with his scrawny features and shocking hairdo.

People walked past, holding their stare that bit longer. Formulating comments as they sauntered; ready to snap them into their phones on the bus home.

'All right?' he went.

'Yup,' I went.

'You all right?' he went to Moya.

She nodded.

I so wanted to thump him.

'Right, come on,' he went to her.

Come on where? Was he the one who liked taking pics? Who liked posting shit about females so the world could mock the fuck out of them?

There were loads out there.

And I should've seen it in her eyes, right there at those school gates.

I didn't understand how scared she was.

I failed her.

I see that now.

Gates

As soon as I exit the art-school gates, my heart starts trying to thump its way out of my body. I hate the feeling. Worrying what I'll find when I get home, what mood she'll be in. Will she be dressed or still strutting about in her misery uniform? Fact: she's scrawnier than ever. Her hairdo is shocking too.

'All right?' I go.

'Yeah,' she goes.

'What did you do today?'

'Don't start, Maggie.'

I want to rattle life into her. For her to come back to me.

If I tell her I've set her up with some unknown, the poor woman will probably think I'm mocking the fuck out of her.

I'm not, you know.

I try to see life through her eyes, how tough it is.

I'm trying to understand her, but my life's tough too.
Why can't she see that?
Who's scared for me, eh?
Have I been failed?

Cousins

Moya wanted us to have landing strips, so she blagged her Aunt Jean's Veet cream and battered round to mine. State of us sitting on the bath was a pure riot, white foam slapped on our crotches. It wasn't as if we were sprouting out of our knickers, but she'd read on some site that all guys preferred landing strips than the full bush. I didn't have a clue what it was until she told me. By fourteen Moya was my very own agony aunt.

'Watch it doesn't go inside,' she went.

'What'll happen if it does?' I went.

'Probably burn the hole off you and you wouldn't be able to do it.'

'What, ever?'

'I'd say for a month at least.'

After scraping the Veet cream off, she squealed.

'Look at it, Mags, it's red raw. Looks like a table-tennis bat.'

'God, so it does.'

Looked like a landing strip all right, with the red lights switched on either side. I nearly fell in the bath laughing.

'Check yours out, it's perfect,' she went.

'It's OK actually,' I went.

'Bitch.'

'It was your idea, Moya.'

'Well, you should've stopped me.'

But I didn't stop her, did I?

The girl always commandeered my room to explore her deepest thoughts. Hands behind her head, pillow on her belly, eyes in search of life's great meaning. I can still see the image of her every time I enter my room.

'Mags?'

'What?'

'If someone had a gun at your head and you had to – mean, you *had* to, no option – would you shag Mr Melrose, Mr Rogan or Mr Glavin?'

'I'd take the bullet.'

'You're not allowed to – you've got to shag one of them, and snog them as well.'

'And what if I say no?'

'Then you have to do the booby prize.'

'Which is?'

'You have to shag Miss Lambert in assembly.'

'I'd rather slash my own throat, Moya.'

'My game, you can't.'

'OK, I'd shag … Mr Rogan,' I went.

'Oh my God, you are a pure slut, Maggie Yates.'

I'd slap her with the pillow; let's just say she got slapped loads.

I still remember one of the last times she barged straight in, flopped herself down, blew out her cheeks and vented. I was at the stage where I didn't give a rat's arse about her latest dickhead boyfriend. I'd no advice or comforting words for her.

'Nikki Morris said she saw him in KFC with some girl,' she went. 'You believe her?'

'Why would she lie?' I went.

'Cos she's a fucking ugly bitch who couldn't get a guy at a gypsy's wedding.'

'She's not that bad.'

'She's an evil cow.'

'What were they doing?'

'Having chicken, I think.'

'What're you worrying about then?' I went.

'Well, he's never taken me to KFC, has he?'

'Maybe it was a relative?'

'Maybe.'

It wasn't just Nikki Morris who spied her latest MOT either. Jade Paget saw him checking out dry shampoo in Boots with some young thing while Rebecca Wade saw him flicking through the Argos catalogue with someone else. He was pure ripping the piss out of Moya, but what could I have said? I might've convinced myself that he'd a glut of young female relatives too. I said nothing in case she blamed me.

'Just, I don't know, just makes me feel bad, that's all,' she went.

'Why not ask him outright?'

'You nuts?'

'Why?'

'He'd think I was a complete psycho.'

She was a complete psycho putting up with that spunk sack.

'How?'

'He'll think I've been stalking him or something.'

'Just say someone saw him – what's the big deal, Moya?'

'He'll go mental, I know him, Mags. He will.'

'Some catch,' I went.

'That's what guys do though, innit? You tell them something they don't want to hear and they go off their rocker.'

I didn't say anything.

'It's not funny, Mags.'

'Who's laughing?'

'He's making me feel like I'm going insane.'

You'd need to be, staying with him.

'Maybe he's not right for you, Moya.'

She leaned on her elbows, glared at me.

'What're you on about?'

'Just that sometimes two people are not right for each other, that's all.'

'We are right for each other.'

'OK.'

'He's said he loves me and I've said I love him.'

'OK.'

'Why is nobody right for me, Mags?'

'We don't know what's right until we feel it, and it's a two-way thing.'

'Well, I've decided that this one is right.'

Aw well, that was it sealed then. I couldn't help her cos she was incapable of seeing through him. She must've read those new comments online, she must've. I didn't want to go there again.

'So, what are you worried about then? Don't you trust his love?' I went.

'Love just makes me feel sick all the time – it comes attached to pain.'

'You're meant to be walking on clouds, Moya.'

'Yeah, maybe my clouds are made of shit.'

Problem with that girl was that she pure fell in love at the drop of her drawers. Had a total love/hate relationship with it.

Anyway …

'Right, what do you want to start with first? Maths, English or biology?' I went.

'Mags, how can you even talk to me about studying?'

'That's why you're here.'

'Can't you see I'm in turmoil?'

'But …'

'Can't you see that?'

'Course I can.'

Back then I couldn't, but now I do.

'Not as if I'm going to pass my exams anyway,' she went. 'Not as if I'm heading to some swanky uni, is it?'

'You never know.'

'Oh, I know.'

We both did.

Covers

(After our disastrous cover of the Rolling Stones's
'Under My Thumb')

'God, we're totally shit,' I go. 'Everyone sounds terrible, apart
from you, Plum. You're dynamite.'

Oh, you're dynamite, Plum. You're the best at everything,
Plum. I want to lick your plums, Plum.

Just don't!

'Come on, we're not that bad, Maggie,' Davis goes. He gets
my glare: eyes squeezed, lips taut. 'Are we?'

'Yes, Davis, we are,' I go. 'Rank rotten.'

'It d-does sound a b-bit shit if I'm being honest,' Alfie
stutters.

'Speak for yourself,' Davis goes.

You never told me I was dynamite at anything.

You're dynamite at being a pain in the arse. How's that?
Go sing.

'We're certainly off-key in the chorus,' Plum goes. 'Which can be easily fixed.'

I point at Davis.

'You have to learn that song properly.'

I turn to his best mate.

'I know I'm not exactly Ringo, Alfie, but there's no need to beat those things to an inch of their life, so cool the jets a bit.'

The guys' heads bow.

Girls sit proud.

'All we need is a bit of finesse. Mean, it's not brain science or anything,' I go.

'More practice is what we need, as a group. Put the time in,' Plum goes, scanning her eyes across the three of us. Is she accusing us of lazyitis? Feel like telling her that some of us don't have a spare trillion hours a week to fiddle around with an orchestra of instruments. SOME OF US – Plum – have to make sure our mums aren't pissing away their days watching repeats of *Wanted Down Under* or dreaming up a food-bank wish list. So, while you're spending your evenings snogging a tuba, that's what I'm doing. Among other things.

'I think it's better if they just learn the songs, Plum,' I go.

'I have an idea,' she goes.

The lads look up.

'I like when you have an idea, chicken,' Alfie goes.

'Oh, thanks, mushroom,' she goes, before remembering that they aren't alone. I can see this band turning into a complete disaster movie before it's even begun. Creative differences, was it? No, some people's love chat made me want to vom.

Davis and I look at each other, trying hard not to howl. I mouth, 'Chicken,' to him. He mouths, 'Mushroom,' to me. Our eyes smile. Wonder what we'd call each other.

'What's the idea, Plum?' I go.

'So, I'm thinking, why doesn't Davis play bass and I play guitar?'

'Can you play guitar?' I go.

Stupid question.

'Classical, but playing pop-song chords will be easier,' she goes.

Pop songs? The Stones? This chick's in need of some serious music education.

'Can you even play bass, Davis?' I go.

'Erm ... don't know.'

'It's easy,' Plum states. 'I can teach you the basics, but you'll need to practise.'

'Brilliant!' Alfie adds. 'We'll be the rhythm section. How cool would that be?'

Davis's body expands, his face sparkles. Just as long as it's the bass she'll be teaching him and none of this chicken and mushroom garbage.

'Yeah, that could work,' Davis goes. 'I'll give it a try.'

And that's how you solve the problem of your band-being-utter-shit. Little tweak here, little tweak there. Obviously, no one says anything to me directly, but I know myself. Time to start gargling the old honey and lemon.

When we're putting the gear away, Davis, Alfie and Plum act as if they're being butchered at the mere mention of our assignment result. I tell them I'm more concerned whether Morrissey's new album will be a three starrer or not.

'My grade means as much to me as seeing a thinner America, Davis,' I go.

'Really?'

Truth: I want a fat red *A* across the page. Yeah, I know, in my dreams. Very least, I don't want anyone thinking I'm a thick waster. Waster bit I can swallow, but the thick part will be hard to squeeze down the gullet. I'm many things, but thicko I'm not.

God's honest: I'm dreading the result dropping; stricken about being some clichéd failure. I do study, work on what I don't understand ... which is almost everything; trying to keep on top of things, fighting with the weight of pressure.

Be nice to go back to my old school in the future, hold up my degree, give everyone a massive get-it-up-you gesture. *'Weep like a newborn, you gaggle of bawbags. And, see this finger? It's from Moya Burns.'*

Maybe the prospect of this first grade has stewed my brain, cos Mum isn't bothering her hole about much these days, least of all how her daughter is coping at art school.

'Good luck with later,' Davis whispers as we leave. I give him a blank stare.

'With what?'

'Telling your mum about the actor lookalike.'

Shit, I totally forgot to google that.

And shit again cos I totally hadn't thought about it, for like twenty-three seconds.

Cheers, Davis.

Mudhoney

My knees are sweaty as I shake the key into the door. I feel nauseous. Think my period's due.

Wish she'd just open the blinds, let *something* sneak into the house. Maybe even free a window; reeks like a cat lover's bungalow in here.

Never know, she might be delighted when I tell her; sometimes you just need to make a tiny change for things to get better. Mean, if the Damp can do it with an instrument swap, then Mum can easily improve thanks to my Ian scheme.

I take a huge intake of rotten air. Open the living-room door.

'Hi, Mum.' My voice oozes positivity. Very un-me.

Silence.

'What've you been doing?' I go.

Apart from thumbing the remote, that is?

'Nothing,' she goes, eyes on the box. Don't even recognise the programme. Some game show. A slipper dangles from one of her feet.

'You been sat here all day?'

'Look, Maggie, get off my case, will you?'

'I'm just asking.'

'Well, don't.'

Her finger frantically taps the arm of the chair; you'd swear she's waiting on her dealer arriving. I glare at her; she glares at the game show. Her finger's got fury in it. Not the perfect conditions to deliver this Ian news, but when would be?

'Hey, want to hear something kinda cool, Mum?' I go, making my way to the curtains.

Kinda cool? Do I even know you?

Not a good time, Moya.

I'm about to split the curtains, twist the blinds, liberate a window, breathe in some fresh. My hands are on them.

'Well,' I go, 'it's just a *bit* cool, but you have to promise you won't get—'

'Just leave them,' Mum goes. 'I want them closed.'

'Just going to let some air in.'

'If I want air I'll go for a smoke.'

'Fresh air I mean.'

I whoosh them open.

'What did I say, Maggie?' she pure screams.

'Calm down, it's only a curtain.'

'Close them.'

I snigger at her.

'Now!' she shoots at me.

I shake my head, crack a mocking smile.

Mum launches herself off the chair. Slipper raised above her head. Eyes on fire.

'What the fuck did I say?'

I cower into the curtains, wait for the slipper to smack my jaw.

'OK. OK. I'll close them. I'll close them.'

I shield myself.

Mum freezes, I freeze. The slipper drops, flops off my head and on to the floor. She covers her face with both hands; her body vibrates. I hear the sniffs, witness the shuddering shoulders, listen to her silent screams. I can't be here, need to bolt.

As I leave she says something, not sure what – think it's 'sorry' or 'worry' or 'blurry', I don't hear properly. It's as if everything's happening in slow motion, all sounds muffled.

So, that went well.

I'm going to my room to be alone. ALONE!

Tom Waits probably isn't the best person to be listening to when your stomach is trying to escape your body. Course I can't blame Tom Waits, I know that, I'm not a total numpty. Isn't his fault, is it? He doesn't help though. Fine, it's my balls-up for putting him on in the first place.

Maybe Mum's slipper incident means she can't change.

Maybe I can't either. We're like pure mud and honey, similar to me and Moya, me and Davis. Me and everyone. Who's who though?

I'm definitely getting an F for this assignment.

I check out music sites, listen to American indie bands for twenty minutes. I watch racists getting attacked on YouTube, which should be joyous but I can't concentrate. See, I know what's coming. I've known all along. I've known since I left Mum bubbling into her hands. Actually, I've known since witnessing her finger hammering that chair and seeing the nothingness in her eyes. Total vacant. God, even her skin looks sad.

They're Mum's scissors.

I know exactly what I'm planning.

Proper hairdresser ones. Expensive. Sharp as anything. Shiny numbers. She won't miss them. I know I'm going to do it; isn't a question of how. I know *how*, duh! More a question of when. She won't dare enter my room after slippergate so the night belongs to me. I'll be staggered if she even makes it to bed.

I don't remember what song it is, definitely something off *Rain Dogs*. I lie down. Cover Larry with the pillow. Can't have any witnesses. Tom Waits's voice enters my world. I focus. Eyes squeezed shut, head bent backwards, listening to Tom's mad, gruff, alkie voice. Lyrics backflip in my blood. I float. I flutter. And then I fly.

In mid-flight, I place metal to skin.

I don't dare look. Don't care how deep or how long I'm cutting. I've zero control; in automatic psycho-chick mode. My deformed conker brain has kicked in. Something seriously wrong with you, girl.

Press.

Pierce.

Pull.

Perfect.

I don't suffer; there's no agony.

Well, nothing that drives up my hips anyway; only teeth-gritting stuff. Can't explain how fantastic the sensation of the fluid running down my inner thigh feels. Warm snakes. Slithering. Trickling. Tickling. My right foot strokes my left. Pleasure or pain? Mud or honey? Choose.

The dribble becomes a flow. The flow becomes a flood. Mr Waits leaves my conker and I return to being Maggie again.

Fuck!

The flood has seeped under my legs, sneaking towards my vag, some behind my knees, dripping on to my sheets. Jesus, Mum'll rip her liver out if she sees the state of them, or will she? Not as if I haven't stained them before with the same: tiny droplets during the night. They remain, a bit crusted now. Those were the early days when I had zero clue. Turns brown as if you've shat the bed.

I'll have to wash them.

There's no airing cupboard stuffed with fresh linen in our gaff; these things will need boiling.

I examine the damage done. I'll have a scar. Pure passion assassin. All imaginary Davis capers will have to be postponed.

I stuff the sheets in the washing machine, two hours at ninety degrees. Domestic goddess.

I look at the mutilation again.

And again.

I'm going to have to bail on Mum, which makes me feel like a baby-abandoner. I'll have to ditch the towel wrapped around my leg in some hospital bin.

Stitches

First they ask, 'Name, address, DOB?'

Next it's, 'What happened, love?'

I spin a total yarn. Then I sit and prepare myself for the ninety-seven-hour outpatient wait.

I'm minding my biz, but can they leave me alone? No chance, they have to send out some batty snoop, don't they; this dowdy, old wreck with bulging boobs trundles towards me. Clipboard in hand, pen behind her ear, ready to do society's duty. Seen her sort before. The social-worker uniform is pure vile. Oversized rags. But durable. Asda, I'd wager.

'Do you want to come with me?' she goes, dead earnest and sincere.

This is about as exciting as hospital waiting rooms get, so of course I go with her. If someone says, 'Come with me,' then you go with them; that's kind of the deal here.

She leads me into a rank room with four chairs and a table. A hospital with no hospitality, what's that all about? I remember it from that time I visited Moya: smells of bogging food and BO. Remove the reek of illness, the anguished faces, the medical staff and we could easily be in a police station. I've done something mind-bogglingly nuts, but it's no crime. Maybe a crime against sanity ... at a push, but not a *crime* crime.

Please, whatever happens, I don't want to go to intensive care. Never again.

'Maggie, isn't it?' she goes.

'Yup.' I'm in no mood for chat.

The temporary bandages are rubbish. Top of my leg is a mess. She catches a glimpse of the inner-thigh carnage and can't hide her sneer of superiority. Some poker player she'd make. Tells me her name's Val, like I care. Tells me she's a hospital social worker. Look at me, Val, do you see someone who honestly gives? Says she wants to get some vitals before I head to the sewing room.

'Want to tell me what happened?'

'I need stitches for this,' I go, pointing to the bloody gap.

'Did you have some type of accident?'

'Yes.'

'Would you like to tell me exactly what happened, Maggie?'

'No one else was involved.'

'I'm not implying that. I just …'

'Why am I here? You can't keep me here.'

'If we think there's a protection issue, I'm afraid we can.' My face drops. Usually I'd throw a wobbly, but I feel weak. 'The phone number you gave as your next of kin is a false one, isn't it?'

'God sake. What is this?'

'We tried it.'

My face drops further, almost smacks off the floor.

'So, I made a mistake,' I go.

'Look, Maggie, unless you provide us with the name of your guardian, we can't allow you to leave this hospital unattended.'

'But I'm old enough.'

'Sorry, but that's just the way it is.'

'Sake!' I tut.

'We have a duty of social protection. Do you know what that means?'

I say nothing, concentrate on my leg.

I can tell Val takes no shit. She's seen it all before, and this shit I'm pedalling isn't the kind she's ever going to buy. She'll just throw it right back at me.

There's no sign that it's coming; it's as if someone inside me has opened the sluice gates. If I'd felt it simmering in my gut I could've stopped it. Closed the bloody gates. But here, alone, in a strange place, in a bit of pain, it pours. I begin to howl. My entire body throbs. I can't stop it. The tears, the noise, the shock. Is it cos I'm back in this place, with all the memories swirling in my head? Or is it cos I'm a complete twat basket? My nose runs. AND THIS EVIL MASCARA!

Val's expression doesn't shift. Some folk are born cold; this chick is positively Baltic.

'Take your time. Here.' She hands me a hanky. No words of comfort. All she wants is my truth-puke. 'When you've calmed down, you can tell me about it.'

She just sits there, saying nothing. Crossing her legs and tongue painting saliva on her lips.

The convulsions stop. Val springs into action.

'OK?' she goes, clicking open her pen. 'Are you ready to talk?'

'OK,' I go.

The air tastes stale.

It's much easier exposing my worries about Mum than telling her about this fucked-up thing I've done to myself. Val's been around these houses too many times, definitely sat across from plenty of cutters in her day. Woman knows the script.

I tell her it was just a game that got out of hand, that I really didn't mean to do it. Her expression thunders, 'Yeah, right!'

'Please don't phone my mum,' I go.

'Maggie, we have to contact someone.'

'Fine, but just not her – she's not up to it.'

'What about Dad?'

'Good luck with that.'

'I see. There has to be someone, otherwise we'll have no other option than to involve social services.'

They can shove that right up their kipper if they think I'm sleeping in some bogging bunk-bed dorm with a throng of abandoned strays. No danger.

'There's Anna,' I go.

Her name just spurts from my mouth; I don't have a chance to think about it.

'Is Anna a relative?'

'She's a sort of counsellor.'

'Your counsellor?'

'Yes.'

'Counsellor for what, if you don't mind me asking?'

I BLOODY DO.

'Grief issues.'

'Grief issues,' she goes, quietly. 'I see.' Val scribbles into her clipboard. 'Do you have a number for Anna?'

She pauses, gawks at me. I check my phone and rhyme it off.

'OK, Maggie, you return to the waiting room and I'll get back to you.'

It's a ten-stitcher job.

The nurse doesn't ask any awkward questions. She knows.

'A tiny bit of muscle damage but nothing that won't heal,' she goes.

The scar isn't in a straight line, it's a squiggle; must have changed direction as I did it. We speak about my school days while thread's being tugged through my skin. I totally invent a different school experience, tell her I was this big grade-A student. Prefect badge on my blazer. Total swot material. And dead sporty.

She asks me about boyfriends; I create this fictitious guy in my life, call him Davis. She says he's a keeper. I even mention the Damp, which seems to impress her. I tell her about the Smiths. She's never heard of them. Really? She's an Adele nut. We don't speak music after that.

I know she wants to ask me; the curiosity is bursting out of her scrubs.

'Just wash it with some saline every night and try to keep the wound clean,' she goes.

'No worries,' I go.

Anna sees me before I see her. She comes forward, arms spreadeagled. God, I hope these people don't think she's my mum. One of those mental feminists who have kids in their late forties. Gran I'd accept at a push, but Mum? Val is standing behind her.

'Everything OK?' Val goes, gesturing towards my stupidity.

'Ten stitches.'

'I've had a chat with Anna and she's going to make sure you get home in one piece.'

'Fine,' I go.

Val says goodbye and ambles down a corridor in search of another lost puppy.

Anna's smile almost cuddles me when I see her. My throat throbs. She wraps her arms around me, holds me tight.

'Oh, my love. What is happening to you?' she goes.

'I just did something weird, something stupid. Sorry,' I go.

'Don't you ever be sorry, my lovely. Don't you ever be sorry.' Her breath is hot on my face. Her clothes smell like a bingo player's. Think she's doused in chemist perfume.

'I'm sorry they phoned you,' I go.

'I'm glad they did, sweetie.'

'I didn't know who else to …'

'It's quite all right.' Her hug gets tighter. 'What are we going to do with you, eh?'

The famous rhetorical question I've had uttered to me, oh, I don't know, about four thousand times.

I don't really remember the walk to the car park.

'Do you need help to get in?' Anna asks as we approach her car.

'I'm not deformed.' I instantly regret saying it. Being a bitch is starting to wear me out.

'OK, I'll let you get on with it then.'

When she turns on the ignition, music blasts out. Tom Waits. I laugh and look at her. Her hand moves to turn it off.

'No, don't. Leave it on,' I go.

'Are you sure?'

'I like it.'

'You know Tom Waits?' she goes, as if I'm some Martian on a day trip.

'I do.'

The bitch in me would've screamed, 'What? Am I not allowed to like Tom Waits?' But I'm totally fed up with her.

'Well, life is full of little surprises, isn't it?' she goes.

'Internet, Anna, that's how I found him.'

'Yes, you're very lucky these days.'

'Don't feel lucky,' I go.

Her hand rests on my good leg.

'These days will pass, Maggie. I know it doesn't seem like that at the moment, but things will get better.'

'Promise?'

It's a stupid question. Wish I hadn't asked it. Silence hangs in the air, apart from Tom Waits's croaking.

When the car pulls up outside our house, all the lights are off. Course they are. Mum's probably still mangled in the curtains, no idea about the whirlpool of waste that's occurred. She'll be sleeping for sure.

'Would you like me to come in with you? Just in case your mum's been wondering where you've been?'

'I doubt she'll be up, Anna.'

'Sure?'

'Sure.'

'OK. Well, you take care, sweetie.'

'I'll try.'

I flick open the car door, swing my duff leg out. The anaesthetic has worn off; stitches sting.

'I hope to see you soon, Maggie, love.'

'OK,' I go, and hobble up my path.

I stop, turn, take a few steps back towards her car.

'Anna?'

'Yes, sweetie.'

'Thanks.'

'Oh, that's OK.'

'And … I just wanted to say … that … erm … I'm really sorry about everything.'

'I told you, you don't have to be sorry to me, Maggie, love.'

'No, I do. I'm sorry about the past few months. For being …'

'Shh,' Anna goes, puts one finger to her lips. 'You take care now, OK?' She smiles.

I smile back.

I inflate my chest, head towards my door.

Ten stitches!

Stupid bitches get stitches.

Results

I eventually drag my bones out of bed, limp to the toilet. My ten-stitcher nips, could be oozing.

Balls, it *is* oozing.

I pull my T-shirt down as far as it can go and hold it taut against my thighs just in case Mum decides to pop out and chase me with a high heel or something. Fat chance that's happening, but precautions still have to be taken. I dab the wound with saline and tepid water, attempting to scrape some dried blood away. Still raw. I pee. Kick my knickers across the floor. I wipe. Then I take the showerhead off its holder and halo it over my head. Some angel I'd make.

I twist the knob all the way to the right. The water batters against my dome and drizzles down my face.

Cold.

Warm.

Hot.

Roasting.

I count to see how long I can suffer the intensity. The scalding. The pain. The third-degree burns. Bald patch will be ripe red. I feel it cooking.

Fourteen seconds.

A new record.

Twist left.

I squeeze cheap food-bank shampoo, Cien, on to my crown. Lather. Jesus, it's sore. Rinse off at a cool temperature cos I'm not a complete masochist. I splat some Cien shower gel on a sponge and do little circles in and around the ten-stitcher. I clean myself underneath. Finish. Prep done. Fresh and ready to face the day.

Bring it on.

Suddenly I remember today's the day we get our group assignment result; excuse me for forgetting, other things have been dominating my napper. We did do *some* work on it in between rehearsing though. Truth: I haven't put my heart into art school with everything else going on. Need to start, know I do. This is my chance. If I can't be my own cheer-leader, who will be? Not her, that's a given.

God, I can just see her pure pissing herself if I get an F. She wasn't exactly cartwheeling with a firework out of her arse when she heard that I'd got into art school. I wish she had been.

I wish.

I wish.

I wish.

I wish she could've been happier for me, cos if the shoe were on the other foot I'd have been delighted. Still, deep down I wouldn't have wanted us to be going to the same place. Not that I thought she'd have cramped my style, I just needed to scream my own words and tell the world: I am here.

What do you mean, you're going to the art school, Mags?

I got accepted – they accepted me.

The art school in town?

Can you believe it?

What about the local college? What about us sticking together?

We'll still be together.

Not if you're in town all the time we won't.

It's a great course, Moya.

It'll be full of wankers who think they're all that.

It's a good opportunity.

Yeah, well, you'll never get a job with some art certificate, will you?

It'll be a degree.

What-the-fuck-ever!

There's a difference, Moya.

You'll be on the dole like the rest of us.

Thought you'd be happy for me.

Course I'm happy for you.

Pure sounds like it.

I'm just not happy for me, that's all.

You're doing your beauty course.

Just wish I hadn't been a complete fucking dunce at school, that's all.

Don't say that.

True though, innit?

But that day the results arrived she wasn't there, was she? No anger. No happiness. No congrats. Now, I'd take any reaction.

I pull on my gear, go get some water for Mum. Why am I the one bringing the bloody olive branch? I sneak into her room. Dark and fusty. What am I expecting, dancing dicks and vodka fountains? The outline of her body under the covers doesn't move. I put the glass down on her dresser with a thud, just so she knows I haven't totally forgiven her.

'Is that you, Maggie?' she croaks.

'I brought you water.'

'Thanks, love.'

Oh, it's *love* now, is it?

She rolls over, heaves herself up on the bed. I hand her the water, which she guzzles. 'I needed that. I've a mouth like an Arab's flip-flop.' I snigger. A little joke. Un-PC but still nice. Her joking makes me feel better. It's basically a sorry, right?

'Want me to open the curtains?' I go.

We both chuckle.

That's basically a reconciliation hug, right?

'No, leave them a bit longer. Is that OK?'

'Course it is.'

And … we're back.

She sits further up the bed. Her pyjama top that once sucked into her frame now drowns her. Humans have a shit-load of bones.

'What's the weather doing?' she goes.

I peek an eye out.

'Well, it's not pissing down.' I scan the grey clouds. 'I'd say it'll probably be a bit clammy.' She groans. People are funny, letting weather determine their mood. 'How are you feeling?' I go.

'Like I've been in a car crash.'

'Want to talk about last night?' I go.

'I'd rather not, if that's OK?'

'Fine.'

'I feel shame.'

'It's honestly fine, Mum. I'd forgotten about it as soon as I went to my room.'

'I didn't hear you that much last night.'

'I slept,' I lie. 'Anyway, it's totally done.'

'OK,' she goes.

'Did *you* get much sleep?'

'I did, but I'd say I could sleep some more.'

'So, sleep some more then.'

'I can't sleep my life away, can I? I need to get up and face the day.'

'Can I get you anything?' I go.

She rubs her cheeks as if she's washing away dead skin.

'Want me to do your eyebrows, Mum?' I ask cos they look like a couple of Brillo Pads trying to flee from her forehead. Can't have her going on a date looking like some bag lady, can I? She runs two fingers along them.

'These?'

'Be nice to do them, no?'

'What's going on, Maggie?'

'Nothing's going on.'

Her eyes squint a bit; she knows this isn't who her loony daughter is.

'You're hiding something.'

'Look, want me to do them or not?'

'Mmm.'

'I'm trying to be nice, remember?'

She feels them again; any longer and they'll have their own ecosystem.

'Last chance,' I go.

'Show me your hands first.'

I fan them out in front of her eyes. Mum inspects for steadiness and control. I excel with flying colours. 'OK,' she goes, 'use the scissors and tweezers.'

I pick up the instruments. I'm good at using scissors.

'Close your eyes,' I go.

'Be careful, Maggie. Make sure they're the same length.'

'I know what I'm doing.'

'Don't thin them out too much.'

'I've got this.'

Comb.

Snip.

Tweezer.

Pat with index finger.

Quick and easy.

'There.' I hold the mirror up to her face. 'What do you think?'

She angles her head. Nods. 'Good job.'

I admire my work.

'You look beautiful now,' I go, which feels weird to say.

'Oh, would you listen to yourself.'

I pure ogle her.

God, underneath that nicotine-aged skin she *is* beautiful. Hard work, but really beautiful. Wouldn't be a red neck walking around town with her if she spruced herself up a notch. Actually, maybe now's the perfect time to say something about this actor lookalike?

Singer

I'm not prancing around pogo-style or karate-kicking an imaginary audience. At rehearsal, I hog the mic stand and chant the Yeah Yeah Yeahs's 'Hysteric' then 'Wave of Mutilation' by the Pixies. I wedge Larry between the stand and the cable, tell the others he's my lucky mascot. The epic Plum sings backing vocals. Girls are totally smashing it, sharing a smile during the 'Wave of Mutilation' chorus.

Even though we're pure chalk and cheese, I'm beginning to really like her; she doesn't say or do much, but when she does it's significant. I've a feeling she has my back, which is all anyone really wants. I'm ready for another gal pal to have my back again. She doesn't care about stage presence; it's all about the tunes for her. Superficial crap isn't important to Plum; she's the person I'm going to show my lyrics to, when the courage comes.

So that's it then, Mags?

What's it?

She just saunters in and you forget all about me?

It's not like that, Moya.

Could've fooled me.

You're easily fooled then.

Look at the pair of you, pure eye-snogging each other.

She's nice. You'd like her.

Someone like that wouldn't give me the time of day.

Oh, please, can you just give me ten minutes? I'm practising here.

Do what you want. I don't give a fuck.

Larry gets launched to where my bag is sitting. Hope the landing's painful.

We go again. But my voice sounds like a strangled cat this time.

Thanks, Moya.

Not listening.

Davis and Alfie have actually struck up a sound that isn't an abomination; they've proper rhythm. Plum has these amazing fingers, like wands. One of these special music-prodigy weirdos. Me? All I have is a voice, and not one that's exactly turning heads in this moment. I don't want to be the weak link, the duffer. The angry one.

They probably think I'm trying to copy Liam Gallagher or Hope Sandoval with the mic stance I'm pulling. Can't really announce I'm doing my best human beanpole cos the ten-stitcher slice on my leg is hindering my movements, can I? I'd rather be anywhere else than standing here listening to the crescendo of shit that's spewing from my gob.

And, yes, I'm blaming you for that, Moya.

Told you, not listening.

I'm wearing a longish skirt with bare legs, harnessing my inner Kate Bush. They told me that letting air into the wound speeds the healing process.

I'm still worried sick about having to tell Mum about this actor lookalike, yet our eyebrow session seemed to alter her mood. Time for another go.

Hope she disowns you.

After rehearsal the others want to celebrate our assignment result – hey, we didn't get that F – but I have to bolt cos I've a date with a sad, old misery puss.

When I finished doing her eyebrows I suggested chips and a walk today, which surprisingly wasn't kiboshed. My attempt at cracking her fear of the outside world – not really. Thought being outdoors would be the best option for dropping the Ian bomb.

Initially she offered to cook, but we both knew that wouldn't be happening. Local chippy then local park it is. Girls' night out. Seriously, I'm using that phrase?

'Can you wear make-up if we're going to be mingling with other humans?' I went, before heading out to practice.

'I'll slap something on.'

'Good woman.'

'I'm proud of you, Maggie. Know that?'

'For what?'

'Well, for being a grown-up for one, and being sensitive. And I'm so sorry about what happened last night.'

'Whatever!' I went, furrowing a brow. Inside I was pure dancing though, dead eager to get to practice … to belt out songs like a drunken handheld hoover.

Girls' Night

So, after rehearsal I breeze in. A bit nonplussed at my performance. I hear pottering from her room. Poke my head around the door; she's sitting on her bed, not putting her face on in front of the mirror like I'd hoped.

'Sweet Jesus, you gave me a fright, Maggie,' she goes.

'That you just shifting?'

'Been napping.'

Her hair is as hostile as my mood. Total firework display.

'Still want to go out?' I go.

She scrunches up her face.

'Can we do it another time?'

Yeah, I'll book you in for my graduation, eh?

Completely predictable.

'Maybe later in the week,' she goes.

'I thought you'd want to show off your new eyebrows?' I tut the head off myself.

'We can make something, if you want. If you don't mind.'

'You want to eat here?'

'Maybe it's best.'

Ordinarily I'd want to brutalise something, show my annoyance; smack her in the face with a pillow, crumple her duvet. But she has me treading shells now so I simply smile in agreement. I don't mind. Mean, the expectation bar was really low anyway.

Do we even have food?

Scavenger hunt is on. I open all the cupboards and the fridge. Utterly depressing. Probably due another food-bank sweep soon. Only allowed three visits every six months though. What kind of system is that? At least we don't need to worry about obesity in our house. Silver linings. I fight my anger; must lock it away before dinner. But I'll have to release it somehow. It's obvious.

My stitches sting, or am I just imagining it?

It'll have to be a stir-fry: chuck the knackered veg into a wok, lob in some noodles and packet sauce, mix well, scoop into a couple of bowls and voila! One slap-up edible feast for two.

It's decided: I'm going to tell her about Ian. The conditions are perfect; the guilt has her all over me – suddenly I'm this pure golden girl. No better time really. Best not to create a bad atmos, Maggie. Put your actor's face on.

When Mum joins me in the kitchen, I morph into full-on waitress mode. Dish towel over the arm; fake smile on the chops. Welcoming eyes. She's fashioned her locks into something acceptable and smeared colour on her jowls. Right, let's all breathe again.

'Can I get you a little something to drink, madam, before you order?' the waitress goes.

'I'll have a sparkling water with a slice of lemon, please,' Mum goes.

'How about lemon-less tap water?' the waitress asks.

'That'll do nicely.'

I pull out the fold-up chair for her to sit on, flap a square of kitchen roll on to her lap. Pour water and set it down.

'Thank you,' she goes.

'Would madam care to order? Or would you like to hear about our specials?' The waitress points to the wok on the cooker.

'And what are the specials today?'

'A noodle stir-fry with far-from-fresh veg.'

'Sounds delicious. I'll order that.'

I drain the noodles and introduce them to the wok. Don't even have a chilli to pimp it up with. Ah, well.

I place the bowl in front of her, plonk one down for myself. I sit. We look at our food. Mum fires me a massive grin. She might be able to widen her mouth, show her teeth, but she can't hide those eyes. A bit pink. I see her trying, but she can't force *them* to smile.

Don't think she has hunger in her tummy. She chases the noodles around the bowl as if trying to knit them into a noodle hat-and-scarf set.

Not much of a girls' night, but there you go.

'Sure you want to be here, Mum?' I go.

'What do you mean, am I sure? Of course I'm sure. Where else would I want to be?'

'Dunno, in bed watching *Love Island?*'

Hold steady, Maggie!

If you want to bring up the subject of Ian in a calm environment, keep everything light and airy, don't assault her chi. How do you even begin a conversation like that though? Can just hear it through a mouthful of stir-fry: 'Oh, by the way, Mum, hope you don't mind, but I've set you up on a date with some dude you've never met before. Don't panic – I've done my homework, he's got no convictions.' Or I could just ask outright: 'Mum, what's your opinion of blind dates?'

'I don't watch *Love Island*, Maggie. I'm more than happy to be here.' She puts her cold hand on top of mine. 'But thanks for looking out for me.'

I'VE ALSO SET YOU UP ON A BELTER OF A DATE! HOW'S THAT FOR 'LOOKING OUT FOR YOU'?

'Who else am I going to look out for?' I go.

'No, I mean it, Maggie. You've been brilliant since this …' She twirls her finger around the kitchen. The universal sign of unemployment fallout. 'I'm proud of you. I want you to know that.'

'Just doing the daughter thing, Mum.'

'I know you've had your own stuff to deal with too.'

'It's no problem, honestly, it's not,' I lie. It's hard to get the words out past the ginormous lump that's living in my throat.

'Still, I'm proud of you.'

'Same goes for me.'

'I haven't done anything to be proud of,' she goes.

'Just ... I don't know ... Getting up every day ... Being on the dole ... It's brave. So, I am proud too. Deal with it.'

Mum looks serious. Deadly serious. She cups both my hands.

'This isn't bravery, Maggie. This is all about trying to stay strong. To not allow myself to sink each day. Bravery doesn't come into it. With everything *you've* been through, you need a mother who's tough and together. I'm just sorry I haven't been that for you lately.'

'You have been,' I go.

Her look softens.

'I'm glad you're holding everything together. It's comforting,' she goes.

I try not to turn my eyes into a guilt-fest; Mum'll clock it right away. One glimpse of my scalp or the state of my legs and she'll know what 'holding it together' really means in our house.

'Come on, eat,' I go. 'I could eat a scabby tramp.'

She raises the glass of tap water.

'Here's to art school, a career as a famous fashion designer and your band.'

'Cheers to that.'

We clink.

'I remember when I applied to study fashion,' she goes, off the cuff.

I almost spit my water all over her foundation.

'You?' I go, as though all mums had no lives before kids arrived to dim the lights on their pasts. 'When?'

'About your age.'

'Really?'

'I got accepted too.'

'You?'

'Yes, me.'

'And why didn't you go?'

'I'm looking at it.'

'Me?'

'Well, not you as such. I got pregnant.'

'That meant you couldn't go?'

'Things were different then, Maggie.'

'Why didn't you go after I was born?'

'Are you kidding? I was afraid to leave you with anyone.'

'What about my dad?'

'He wasn't much help, was he?'

'So, you didn't go to study fashion because of me?'

Another notch on my I've-ballsed-everything-up-for-everyone belt.

'No, not because of you, because of circumstances. I wanted to look after my baby girl more than study fashion, that's all.'

There's no way I'd have done that, no danger. Far too selfish for that palaver.

'You were the most beautiful thing I'd ever seen.'

'Mum!'

'You were, and you still are.' Then her voice brakes and stutters. 'Look at you. You're so beautiful.'

Seriously, can't beat a girls' night out. In.

'Yeah, well, you did a top job, didn't you?' I go, circling my 'so beautiful' face.

'We did OK, Maggie,' she manages to get out. 'I just wish I could've done better.'

'We're more than fine.' I'm stacking up the lies now.

'I just hope you get what you want in life.'

'I'm going to be a top fashion designer, aren't I?'

'I'm scared you're bottling everything up, that you won't be able to look after yourself.'

'What are you talking about, Mum?

'Just doing my actual job, worrying about *you*.'

'Crap that it's unpaid though.'

'That's what parents do, they worry about their children. You'll know when you're a mother yourself.'

'Er … no thanks.'

We both play with the food. Our taste buds aren't interested.

'Any nice guys at art school you've got your eye on?'

Zero chance I'm going down that road with her.

'Erm, no,' I go. 'Haven't been looking, just getting my head down and working.'

Davis pops up on my mind projector. I feel my face burning. Shit, he's naked in the images. I'm not.

'Well, if and when you do find someone, make sure you'll both be careful?'

'Can we change the subject please?' I stuff a forkful into my gob, hoping it'll silence her. Still, I guess her taking an interest in my non-existent sex life is a kind of progress, even if slightly humiliating.

She hasn't made a dent in my culinary masterpiece. Two mouthfuls at most.

Time to draw my gun; she's the one talking about guys and boyfriends, not me. It's the perfect time to tell her about the actor lookalike. FFS, what's his name? It would give her a better idea of what's ahead of her. A bit of context. Something to get excited about. I can even help get her ready for the big date. Style her. Pick out cool gear.

I've tortured myself on how to approach it. How to spin around before getting to the core of the topic. Best just to blurt it, isn't it?

'Mum?'

'What?'

'I've got something to tell you.'

She releases the fork and leans back in her chair.

'What?'

'Promise you won't get mad or batter me with your slipper?'

'I said I was sorry about …'

'I'm joking. I'm joking.'

'Not funny.'

'Just promise you'll listen,' I go.

'Oh, I've a feeling I'm not going to like this, Maggie …'

Her face reads, 'Oh, for the love of hell, I'm going to be a grandmother.'

'Don't worry, I'm not up the duff or anything like that.'

'Well, that's a relief. For a moment I thought …'

'Promise you won't go mental.'

'I promise I won't get mad.'

'No, not *mad*. Mental. Promise.'

'OK, I promise I won't go mental.'

'Shake on it.'

I extend my hand. We shake.

'Tell me.'

I stare at her, try to hit her with my needy face. Little puppy-peepers. She doesn't buy it. Here goes:

'I've set you up on a date.'

Long pause.

Her eyes sink into mine and narrow.

'You've done what?'

'Read this.'

I slide my phone across the table with the email exchange on display; watch her read. Is that steam billowing out her ears?

202

Tear gas actually.

Nostrils flare.

'Maggie, what is this? I can't …'

She puts her palms up to me as she slips out of the chair; plants a cigarette between her lips. I say nothing. Best to let her digest my Cupid routine in peace. Hoping she won't completely fruit her loop when the fag is finished. I'm thinking that I should go for an unneeded piss or something, but I don't. I sit there. Frozen and terrified.

She's at the back door, puffing furiously; short, rapid drags. The smoke swirls around her head as if she's some rock goddess. I wish.

'I can't believe you would dare try to control my life like that,' she goes without even looking at me.

'I was just trying to help, to do something nice for you.'

'Nice?'

'Yeah, nice.'

'What you've done is vindictive and cruel – anything but nice.'

God, you try to do something good for someone and that's all the thanks you get?

'I'm just worried about you, Mum, and I …'

'You think I'm incapable of organising my own life?'

I brave the smoke cloud and move towards her. She lights up another. Turns her eyes to meet mine.

'Get away from me. I can't even look at you.'

'I'm just trying to joy you up a bit.'

'By humiliating me?'

'I want you to be happy, Mum.'

'You've a funny way of showing it.'

'I just thought …'

'Thought what, Maggie? That some man can help me? That some man can just wander in here and fix me like that?' She snaps her fingers together, then chucks the half-smoked fag away. Her voice breaks. So does mine.

'But it's true,' I go.

'What is?'

'That I only want you to be happy. Can't you see that?'

She wipes her eyes and rubs snot away from her mouth, then brushes past me, sits at the table again, pushes the dinner away. She claws her hand through her hair.

'Mum …'

'Is this how you treat me, Maggie?'

My stomach's on a spin cycle loaded with regret. I sit across from her. She pure boots me under the table, catches me right on the side of the foot. Quite like it. Pain travels fast. I don't flinch. Not even sure she meant it. Oh, she meant it all right.

'Hey, that was sore.'

'Good!'

'I thought you'd be happy.'

'Happy?' she sniggers.

'Intrigued at least. God, I won't bother next time.'

'Next time? There won't be a next time.'

'Well, whatever.'

'You're so naive at times, Maggie, know that?'

Now I want to hook her on the face. Floor the ungrateful bitch.

'And you're miserable at times, know that?' I go. 'In fact, you're miserable all the time.'

She exhales loudly. Covers her eyes. Is she crying? Have I made her cry? She better not be; she better not be laying this on me.

'You don't see it, do you?' she goes.

Her voice is shuddery, throat husky.

'See what?'

'What's glaring at you.'

Sounds like she's been gargling glass. I'm confused.

'So, tell me,' I go.

'Have you heard me crying in my room?'

'Course I have.'

'Seen that I can't be bothered doing anything?'

'Yeah.'

'I mean *anything*: getting up, going out, washing, speaking to people?'

She reaches for my hand; mine is muggy, hers is cold. Her jaw is quivering.

'I know it's been hard with the job and all that, but I was—'

'It's more than that, Maggie.'

'Mum, you're scaring the shit out of me. What's this about?'

Suddenly my mind drifts to Moya. And now my jaw quivers. I see tears forming in her eyes. Puddles. I see them through my own.

'Mum, I don't want to be left on my own.'

'That's never going to happen, Maggie.'

'I can't have anyone else leave me again. I can't.'

'Maggie, I'm not—'

'You can't leave too.'

I'm panting so much, struggling to get air into my lungs.

'I'm just trying to tell you that I'm in a very dark place at the moment. A place I can't seem to get out of. I know I need help, I know I do, but this Ian person isn't the way out for me. He's not the help I need.'

'You don't know that.'

'How can I bring some man into this world?' She gestures to herself.

'We all need someone, don't we?'

'I can barely function being with myself. I can't even think about the next five minutes, never mind another person.'

'What can I do then?'

'Just do what you've been doing. Work hard. Find your own way. You're doing an amazing job.'

I'm doing a WHAT job?

Who's failing to see what's in front of them now?

'Life's better if we're both happy,' I go.

'I know it is, Maggie. And I'm working at it, I really am.'

'So am I.'

We wipe our eyes. She gets up, and I think she's coming to hug me, but she stretches and yawns.

'Let me wash up,' she goes.

'You go lie down or watch telly or something. I'll do it.'

'Thanks, love.'

I have my excuse.

Another reason to inflict something upon myself.

Cos this knot in my chest needs untangling.

PART TWO

Likes

We can't tune our brain to everything, can we? Sometimes it's only when we stop and reflect that we recognise what's facing us; when you're directly in its core you can be totally blind.

Now, I want to whip myself, but then I just couldn't be doing with Moya's personal woes. I hate myself for swatting away her problems. For not swallowing the bile she spouted.

'So, I posted this photo on Insta and I only got ten likes. Can you believe that, Mags?' she went.

'Erm …'

'Mean, even Ginger Gilmour gets more than ten likes, and he'd shag the hole in a dolphin's head. Know what I mean?'

'What are you on about, Moya?' I went, cos really I didn't have a clue. She just pure stormed into my room, hurled my

French verbs textbook off the bed and hijacked my space. Again.

'I posted a photo …'

'What photo?'

'Of me and him.'

'Doing what?'

'What do you mean, "doing what?" We were taking a selfie. What do you think we were doing?'

'I don't know, do I?'

'Sake, Mags,' she went, as if I was grilling her.

'OK, I get it, you were taking a selfie. And what?'

'What do you mean, "and what?"'

'Sake, Moya.'

'Sake, you.'

'Just tell me about the fucking selfie.' I was going to finish the sentence with 'and then piss off home'.

'So, I posted it,' she went.

'And?'

'And no one has commented or anything. *He* hasn't even liked it.'

'He hasn't?'

As if I cared about what that dickbrain liked.

'No, but he's commented and liked other people's photos, hasn't he?'

'Why's that bad?'

'Mags,' she went, almost growling at me. 'It's bad. It just is. Forget it – you don't understand.'

'I thought you were getting on OK.'

'We are. I mean, we do. We kind of … oh, I don't know. It's just complicated sometimes.'

'Maybe he's not who you thought he was.'

And without as much as a beat she went:

'But he could be in love with me, Mags.'

I swithered.

Should I have laughed or told her to cop herself on?

'You're allowed to think that,' I went.

'I do.'

Then I chuckled.

'He's a decent guy when you get to know him,' she went.

'I'm fine for getting to know him, but thanks.'

She continued to look through her phone, pure torturing herself, her face contorting whenever someone or something popped up she didn't like.

'And, anyway, what do you care?' she went.

'What?'

'You'll be fannying about with all your new art-school buddies.'

'I haven't even been accepted yet, Moya.'

'So, you will be. Then you'll bugger off.'

'What's that got to do with your boyfriend or anything?'

'Well, at least I'll have someone here, with me, when you do piss off.'

'God, I'm not going to Australia, and nobody's pissing off.'

'Yeah, we'll see,' she went.

'Yeah, we will see,' I went.

'Yeah, we will.'

I let her get the last word in. We'd have been at it all night otherwise.

For the next twenty minutes we didn't speak, she grunted and puffed her way through that phone; think she was trying to hold in the tears. Looking back, it's easy to believe that was the case. But, who knows? Her guts could've been grinding away at her or she could've been totally fine. Who knows?

Visitor

I don't hear the knock on my bedroom door cos Stella Donnelly is blaring out the speakers.

'What is it?' I go.

My organs hit the ceiling when Mum pops her head into my room. She's supposed to be out. First time in weeks she's hit the streets after dark. I'm not raging with her though. Actually I am. Mean, I could've been doing some serious bare-arse boxing with Davis. God, can you imagine? You'd need a hospital visit to have all that red removed from my neck.

'I did knock, Maggie.'

'I'd music on.'

'I just wanted you to turn it down a bit, that's all,' Mum goes, easing herself into the room. She's dolled up, nothing tarty. Skinny chic. Bet Mum could still turn heads. Have men pure seeping out of their jeans.

'Done,' I go, turning the music down.

'Now we can hear ourselves.'

'You're back early,' I go.

'Yeah, film wasn't up to much.'

'Told you Gerard Butler films are worse than torture, didn't I?'

'In fairness, you did.'

'Life's too precious to waste it on him.'

We both nod in agreement.

'Did I hear you speaking to someone?' she goes.

'Oh, that's Davis – he's in the toilet.'

You'd think I'd just handed her the winning lottery ticket. The ultimate happy pill.

'Davis!'

'He's from art school.'

'Art school!'

'He's also in the band.'

'Oh, he's in the band too!'

'OK, OK, don't wet yourself, he just came around so we could try out a few new songs,' I go. 'It's nothing like that. Totally not my type.'

He actually came around to salvage my singing voice, hoping his skills could tune me up. I'd say he could tune me up all right ... Stop it, Maggie! If he even attempts to remove his fingers from that guitar then ... then I'll ... I'll ... tell him he's ... he's ... Oh, I don't know, do I?

I flop back on to the bed and resume my daydreaming

position. Mum shuffles beside me. She reeks of perfume. Those pills must be working wonders. Her essence seems relaxed.

'You thinking of her, Maggie?' Mum goes, out of the blue.

Can she read my mind or something? Some sort of witch, is she?

'I'm always thinking of her.'

'Terrible for anyone to go through that.'

'People just don't see the destruction they leave behind or the stress they cause.'

'No, they don't,' she goes. 'But at least you were there for her, Maggie.'

'Maybe in here, in this room, but not in general.'

'If you ever had feelings like that, you'd tell me, wouldn't you? If you were being trailed, for example?'

'It's trolled, Mum. It's called trolling. God, do you live in a cave?'

There's a glow to her. Not like a few weeks ago when she was moping around in her pyjamas looking like a shadow for hire. But this thing she has is complicated. One day she's shafts of sunshine. Next day sheets of rain. It's starting to confuse the life out of me. And, where is she suddenly getting all this money from to go out gallivanting? Welfare back pay?

'But, really, how are you?' she goes, all timid voice. She never asks me this. Her level of concern has rocketed; she's up to something, I know it.

'I'm good. Just dealing,' I go, cos it's the truth.

I can tell she's hankering for a mad heart to heart. A full-on mother–daughter chinwag. I'm happy when Davis returns from the bog.

'Oh, hi, Mrs Yates,' he goes. 'How are you?'

His voice wobbles – aw, he's nervous. Bless!

Better than sounding like a pure lick-arse though.

Is his 'How are you?' another way for him to say, 'Are you getting over your mental spell, Mrs Yates?' I might have mentioned that she was struggling. I might have mentioned it so he'd feel sorry for me. I might have mentioned it so all his attention would be drawn towards me. Well, he's here, in my room, isn't he? Job done.

'Mum, Davis. Davis, Mum,' I go.

Mum climbs off the bed. Classy.

'Hi, Davis, very nice to meet you,' she goes.

They shake hands.

FFS, do we all have to curtsy next?

The two of them stare at each other. Talk about awkward. 'Right, I'll leave you two to the music then. We'll be in the kitchen if you need anything. Keep it down a bit though, OK?'

'OK, night,' I go.

Meaning don't bother us again.

'Night,' she goes.

'Night,' Davis goes, giving Mum a stupid wave on her way out. If we were actually boyfriend–girlfriend I'd call him a dick with a punch, then envelop him by playing a game of human rash.

Davis fumbles around my music; he better not balls up my alphabetical order.

Larry's sitting on my pillow, judging; I yank him to my chest, hug him until his button eyes bulge. Sometimes I just want him to be my Larry again and nothing else. Can cuddly toys be exorcised?

You told her, didn't you? Moya goes.

Told her what?

You did – you told your mum that that rocket did the dirt on me, didn't you?

I told her nothing, Moya.

Well, she was giving me the pure pity eyes.

Rubbish.

Pity eyes! Mum's haven't been that way for weeks now. Sad, sunken and full of suffering, yes. But not lately.

You're making my life sound like a reality TV show, Mags.

Me?

You know what I mean.

Look, I'm sorry your boyfriend turned out to be a dick ten times over, but some of us have other things on our mind right now.

Layers of guilt smother me, but what could I have done? Honestly, what the fuck could I have done?

I pick up my phone and type 'school bully gets battered' into YouTube. Watch one video for twenty-nine seconds. Some loudmouth gets smacked and falls to the ground like a sack of spuds. Davis puts Young Fathers' new album on.

'This OK?' he goes.

'Fine.'

'You OK?'

'I'm OK,' I go. 'You?'

'Yeah.'

'Did you think Mum was dressed like a tart?' I ask him.

'Erm … not really … erm … I thought she was dressed nice … but I didn't really notice.'

'Sure you didn't. You had your pure MILF radar on. Don't lie.'

Poor guy looks totally mortos. I don't push it. Why do I do this?

Then I remember:

'Did she use the word "we" before she left?' I ask him.

'Eh?'

'As in "we'll be in the kitchen"? She said that, right?'

'That's cos there are two of them in there,' Davis goes.

'How do you know?'

'I saw him when I was coming back from the bog.'

'*Him?*'

'Him.'

'Not *him* him?' I go.

'The very him.'

'Sure it was him?'

'Hundred per cent.'

'Really?'

'Really.'

'No way?'

'What?'

'Nothing, I just can't get my head around it, that's all.'

'Well, I think you'd better.'

'What do you think they're doing?' I go.

Davis shrugs.

We open the door and listen a bit.

'Relax – they're just having cup of tea,' he goes.

'How do you know?'

'Heard the kettle.'

We finish our snoop.

I switch Young Fathers off and sit on the bed beside Davis. Have myself some thinking time; unsure how I feel about some interloper cutting about my gaff, slurping tea and tearing into our dry biscuits.

We all know what he'd like to be tearing into, don't we?

I really want Mum to be normal for once. I do. Loosen her shoulders.

I thought it was just an innocent night out at the flicks and then back to separate homes. Who was I kidding?

Mean, I'm the one who instigated all this make-Mum-happy claptrap and now, when she's the balls to wrap her arms around it, I've a face on me like a singleton on prom night.

After Mum dropped the depression bombshell, she took herself to the doctor; a couple of weeks after that she asked for Ian's details.

'I need that poor man's number, Maggie,' she went.

'Why?'

'To apologise.'

'For what?'

'For having a ridiculous daughter. This is someone's life you're mucking around with here, not some teenage house-party fling.'

Honestly, she really needed to stop believing she's still in the nineties. And stop watching repeats of *Friends*, too.

'What, you're just going to pure phone him?' I went.

'That's exactly what I'm going to do.'

'Mum ...'

'Tell him it's been all one big misunderstanding.'

She was calling my bluff, I knew it. 'Give me the number,' she went, flipping her fingers at me to come across. 'Give.'

I handed it over. *Let's see who's calling whose bluff.*

And know what she did? She only went and called it. I thought I was going to have a mad eppie.

'Hello, is that Ian I'm speaking to?' she went. 'Hi, my name's ...'

I ran into the next room, couldn't take it. Sat behind the door like someone off those Childline ads. Trying not to eavesdrop, yet totally eavesdropping.

I heard

her speak,

listen,

chuckle.

'Oh, I know ... what are they like ... mmm ... well, you must see it in your job all the time ...' Chuckle chuckle. 'No,

I'm not in the frame of mind at the moment to start anything new … mmm … mmm … no, it's not that … well, actually it is … mmm … mmm …' Chuckle chuckle. 'Mmm … mmm … job loss … mmm … oh really?' Chuckle chuckle. 'Well, the one I have is feisty enough …' Chuckle chuckle. 'Good intentions, absolutely … Oh really? Mmm … that's interesting … I guess it's more popular than we think … mmm … mmm … that might work … let me consult my diary …' Chuckle chuckle. 'Mmm … mmm … perfect … and I'm sorry once again … yes … mmm … me too … OK, thanks, Ian … bye … bye … bye.'

Unbelievable. God, adults, who'd be one?

So, a couple of coffee dates later, one park walk and a trip to the flicks (well, half trip) and here he is sitting slurping a hot brew in our kitchen and blethering away with my big chick.

Obviously, I put the Smiths on. The moment's crying out for them; crank up the volume cos I don't want to hear them. Need to cocoon myself. I wanted this to happen, for her to be happy, to glow. They get on brilliantly, I can smell it. And it's all my doing. So why am I suddenly feeling that she's going to piss off into some corduroy sunset with him? Leaving me to fend for myself, living off stir-fries and cheap, shit mascara. She can't. I've no cuddly toy to replace her. I'm delighted she's able to see what a sunset looks like though. God's honest. I'm just being a selfish cow, again.

So, what's new?

Shut up, you.

'I wish I could remember the name of that actor,' I go to Davis.

'Let's look it up.' He bounces off the bed, pulls out his phone.

'Davis?'

'What?'

'Can I ask you something?'

'Sure?'

He's standing in front of me. Three steps away.

'Do you think I can sing, like really sing?'

'I think you've a brilliant voice, Maggie. Unique.'

'Seriously?'

'Seriously.'

'Cheers, that means a lot.'

I turn three steps into two. My body is shaking; feels like my hair is sweating. I don't blink. Neither does he.

'Davis?'

'Yeah.'

'Do you think you could give me a hug?'

Two steps become one. He doesn't move. Please shift, Davis. Just a toe. Give me something to dive on to.

We freeze.

'Erm, I guess I could,' he goes, clumsily opening his arms.

I do the same. Taking another half step.

We're like a couple of cumbersome dancers at a school disco.

And it happens; we hug. Virgin magnets.

My head sinks into his neck; I could wet-lip his skin.

His hands belt my waist, few centimetres lower and he'd be on my arse. I'd let him. I want that.

I tighten into him.

Surely he can feel me against his chest? I've got some. He must feel them.

My breathing heats his cheek.

I want him to grow; I want to sense it on my hip, my stomach, the top of my leg. Should I just go for it? Just cash everything in?

But he'd love that, wouldn't he? Slaggie Maggie, he'd love that. No, don't think I'll be giving you that green light, Davis. Not tonight. Not yet.

'Thanks,' I go, pulling away. 'I just needed a hug.' I give him the tiniest of pushes. May as well have been a sledgehammer though. His eyes! Shit, I've hurt him.

'Erm … yeah. Well, we all do sometimes.'

I return to being three steps away. And suddenly we're two ice sheets drifting apart. God, weirdness is so painful.

'Want to do another song?' I go.

'I think I'd better shoot – it's getting late, Maggie.'

'Yeah, yeah, of course.'

Think I want to cry, not in front of him. But I know he knows. Told you, he's not thick.

'Probably see you tomorrow then,' I go.

'You will.'

225

I lie next to Larry on the bed. Larry gets how I'm feeling. And I get her. I really do get her.

You OK, doll?

Yeah, I'm OK.

I get up in a raging mood, fuming that Mum brought Ian back to the house and didn't even introduce us. I can hear her float about the kitchen. Clinks the spoon off her mug three times, which she never does. Thinks she's making sweet music, total liberty. Obviously, she's buzzing off some kind of post-sex thing. I don't know what that feels like, but that's what she's doing.

Is this how it works? One cock and all your misery sails away? That it? Maybe I do need to try it then.

When I go into the kitchen, I'm fishing for a fight, feel it in my bones. I want to show my displeasure, have a proper old-time barney. There's something wrong with me.

'Morning,' she goes, face ripe, sunbeam wide.

'There's no food,' I go, opening and slamming cupboards.

'I didn't get a chance to go out, Maggie.'

'What, too busy watching *Loose Women*, or being one?'

'Excuse me!'

'Whatever, I don't give a—'

'I don't need this now,' she goes, popping two pills into her mouth.

'Yeah, you never need it. But I need food.'

'There's a tin of soup in there.'

'For breakfast? Fuck sake.'

'What was that?'

'Nothing.'

'Thought so.'

I leave, making sure I slam the kitchen door hard behind me.

'Fuck sake,' I go again.

'I heard that, you know.'

Middle-finger the door.

Getting Better

I curl up with Larry, listen to 'Hotel Yorba' on a loop, play it dead loud to annoy Mum's peace. Won't be long until those pills take control and she'll be zombiefied in the living room anyway.

I gently kiss Larry's string mouth.

Let her be happy, Mags.

How can she be happy when I'm not?

It's what you wanted for her.

You're right.

As per.

It's just hard, Moya, you know?

Just screw the nut, girl. Promise?

Promise.

I don't cry. And, even though my conker's thrashing and pushing me in that direction, I don't hurt myself.

Still, maybe these selfish thoughts need to be punished?

1

I don't punish; stare at the wall instead.

2

Improvement.

3

I hate myself sometimes.

4

But I'm getting better.

5

I must be.

6

I don't draw blood.

7

So, I must be.

8

No yanking clumps of hair.

9

Really, I must be.

10

I'm pure poison.

But I'm getting better.

I don't hurt myself, so I must be.

Fashion

Mum slips me twenty quid out of her 'incapacity benefit' as a kind of look-how-I'm-getting-better and sorry-for-everything gift. She must be stashing away her social payments.

'Buy yourself something nice in town, Maggie,' she goes.

Twenty quid to buy some new gear? I don't have the heart to tell her that twenty quid won't get you anywhere near a Topshop till. But, still, twenty quid's twenty quid. Burger King or Primark?

Lee Alexander McQueen won't be rigging me out with my twenty spons that's for sure.

I love shopping for clobber, but it's no barrel of laughs, standing in your bra and knickers surrounded by a three-way mirror. Every flab, flop, droop, stretch mark and scar on show to combust your self-esteem.

Worst part? Never having enough to buy the things you like.

It's my first solo spree; talk about stress. She was brutally honest when I asked for her opinion:

'What do you think of this, Moya?'

'You can actually see the cellulite in your arse through that.'

'What about this then?'

'A jumpsuit! Seriously?'

I gave mine also:

'This too short, Mags?'

'You'd see your knickers if you bent down.'

'Not a bad thing.'

'I'd maybe go for a bigger size.'

When I return from town, Anna's car is sitting outside our gaff. Small silver thing. Pensioner's run-around. I haven't seen her since our A & E meeting, which was ages ago now. Naturally I cack it. Big time. Seeing her car is like a hammer to the forehead. Is she playing nosy bugger? Is she spouting everything she knows to Mum? My sick mum. How sick is that? What does she want? Does patient confidentiality mean bugger all to her?

They're drinking tea.

I smell ginger as soon as I open the door. Anna stands up, heads towards me with outstretched arms. Her lips smack my cheek.

'Oh, it's lovely to see you, sweetie. Just lovely.'

Anna looks at Mum, who I know has had a doctor's appointment that very morning. Mum smiles. My legs jelly up.

'What's so lovely?' I go.

Have they found a cure for Mad Mum Disease?

'You're a singer in a pop group?' Anna goes.

I want to uppercut her, leave her sprawled out on the rug. Pop group? Inconsiderate cow. Has she met me? Pop group! How dare she? I muster a grin. Can't believe Mum would've mentioned anything about that to her.

'Yeah, it's good,' I go.

WHAT ARE YOU DOING HERE, ANNA? IN MY HOUSE? WE DON'T LIKE VISITORS OR INTRUDERS. SO, DO ONE! GO ON, BLOW THE SCENE.

Anna gives me one of those you-don't-need-to-worry-your-secret's-safe-with-me looks.

Let's not unfurl our bras here, shall we?

She comes in for a tight hug. Me and Mum exchange our this-is-a-bit-weird eyes. I want Mum to give me a cheesy grin, let me know we're on the same page, but she doesn't.

'I was just passing this way and thought I'd pop in to see how my favourite girl was getting on.' God, she makes it sound as if I'm a pug.

Our bodies part.

'I'm doing good, Anna,' I go.

NOW BEAT IT.

'Oh, you must be very proud of her talents, Donna.'

'I am, Anna,' Mum goes.

'And you must be very proud of yourself, my darling,' Anna goes to me. 'Social activity is a step in the right direction.'

I shrug.

She is still talking about the band, isn't she?

'Oh, it is Anna,' Mum goes. 'She just doesn't want to appear big-headed about her singing voice, that's all.'

'Your mum and I have been having a lovely chat, Maggie.'

KNEW IT! COULDN'T KEEP YOUR TRAP SHUT, COULD YOU?

'And?' I go, looking at my two conspirators. Mum's pruned eyebrows shoot up and down.

'And we feel that it's important for you to begin a new course of meetings with me, if you wanted to. I've spoken to the powers that be, and they agree. It'll be through the health board, so there's no cost.'

I look at Mum for support.

'Do I have to?' I go.

'Entirely up to you, sweetie.'

'It's your decision, Maggie.'

They both pure corner me.

'But I thought we'd finished, like I'd passed that stage now.'

They look at each other as if I'm an hour away from a straitjacket.

'Well, you could see it that way, but we feel, Donna and I, that there is still a way to go,' Anna says. 'But, as I said, it's up to you.'

'It's a busy time for me, with art school and the band and …' I'm about to say 'with Mum', but I leave that one hanging.

'No, I fully understand that, sweetie, that's why we would structure it around your schedule.'

Anna looks directly at me like she doesn't want to let the thigh-slashing cat out of the bag. Is this a threat? God, is she blackmailing me?

'It might help you settle with things, feel calmer, less stressed,' Mum goes. 'It's always good to have another ear instead of just me and the people in your band.' She coughs loudly, followed by three wet sneezes.

STRESSED? WHO'S STRESSED?

'I really think it'll be a good thing,' she adds, then pushes herself up to fetch a hanky from the kitchen.

With Mum out of the way, Anna takes a step closer.

'How are you doing, love?' she whispers.

'Fine,' I whisper back.

'Is your leg healing?'

'Totally healed.'

'That was a nasty one you gave yourself there.'

'It's fine now.'

'Well, I'm glad you're on the mend. I was worried.'

'You haven't said …'

'Don't fret, I haven't told your mum a thing. That wouldn't be advisable under the circumstances.'

I swallow some saliva. Tense my toes.

'Thanks,' I go.

'But I do think you should come and see me though – we really do need to keep up our sessions.'

I say nothing.

'Will you at least think about it?'

I plant myself on the couch.

'I'll think about it,' I go, only to get the pain off my arse.

Mum returns, sniffing mightily into her hanky.

'Maggie's going to think about it, Donna,' Anna goes.

'It'll be for the best, Maggie.'

Before Anna bolts, she and Mum come together; they hug for pure ages. Also, I'm sure Anna breathes something into Mum's ear and vice versa. When they part, I notice their glazed eyes. Mum's have been glazed for a good few weeks now, but it's strange to see Anna's eyes setting themselves up for a downpour. Mean, all the stuff she's heard from me and not as much as a trace of a tear. Not one drop. Strange.

Then she's chugging off in her little car. Tom Waits booming no doubt.

'Would you do that for me, Maggie?' Mum goes.

'I just want to forget certain things,' I go. 'Going to Anna brings it all back – can you not understand that?'

'Of course I can. But seeing her makes sense.'

'I don't—'

'Just try a few weeks, see how you get on. Anyway, you might not be able to do it if your schedule doesn't suit.' Not getting angry around Mum can be a chore so I scrunch up my face. 'Do it for me, Maggie?'

God, this is emotional blackmail. These people should come with a warning. It's all very cultish. I should be recording these chats for future court dates.

'But just a couple of weeks and then that's it; I'm done after that.'

'Do a few sessions at least.'

'Can't wait.'

In the good old days Mum would've thrust a finger into my cleavage and said something like, 'You're going and that's the end of it. No ifs, no buts – you're doing it.' These days it's all pleases, thanks yous and kind requests. Depressed and medicated Mum is a pure joy.

'How did it go with the doctor?' I go.

'Fine.'

'Fine, how?'

'What did you buy?' she goes.

'Jeans, pair of tights, a shirt, a T-shirt and a hat.'

'All for twenty pounds?'

'I'm a bargain hunter, Mum.'

'I'll say.'

'So, the doctor?' I ask again.

Mum's phone beeps.

Beep!

Beep!

Beep!

She glances over the text, trying hard not to snigger; her eyes fizz though. I clock them. She puts her hand on her belly like she's pregnant; subtle, but I clock that as well. Acting as if she's just gulped down a big gust of air. Her chest heaves upwards. Her mouth's wet with all her lip-licking. She does know I'm still here, doesn't she? Does she even give a shit?

I know fine well who's beeping her and making her all giddy.

I'm not an eejit.

Thankfully it's not only the happy pills that have got her all optimistic and goo-goo lately.

Without shifting her eyes from the phone screen she goes, 'Right, you best get those new clothes upstairs then,' and makes her way back to the living room.

'Mum?' No answer. 'Mum?' I semi-raise my voice. She turns, lifts her head.

'Yes, Maggie?'

'You didn't answer me.'

'Didn't answer you what?'

'I asked what the doctor said?'

Her phone hand drops to her side and she reverts back to old Mum mode: schoolteacher stance, fierce facial expression. The works.

'Oh, you know. She's happy with my progress.'

'Well, that's good, isn't it?'

'I suppose it is.'

Phone

She'd sit there, scowling, scrolling from picture to picture, comment to comment. Totally obsessed with what they'd posted, muttering all these deranged things under her breath. Trying to put faces to their judgements. I tuned out. Couldn't be arsed getting involved.

Ping

Night after night she sits howling at the screen. Thing pings and her face illuminates; totally obsessed with his WhatsApps. She sniggers, constantly muttering mushy stuff under her breath. Don't want to judge her too harshly; I'm delighted for her, I am, but can't be arsed with all the love-struck vom of it all.

Teeth

Brushing my teeth, listening to the crunch of the brush, I'm thinking about it. Playing that night over and over in my head. God, that night! I can't get her face out of my thoughts. And I brush. Hard. Thinking. Brushing. I spit pink into the sink. But don't stop.

Scrub them, Maggie. Scrub them hard.

Her words still echo from that night. 'I should've hunted them all down, cut their balls off when I had the chance, Mags.' They continue to hover, pure penetrating me. Maybe I should've been part of the hunting party. Blew it!

I scrub.

Spit.

Red hits the basin.

Still too pink though; needs to be deeper. Darker. No, not red. Like crimson. The real-deal stuff.

I didn't help her.

Some pal I was.

Failure friend.

I almost bite the toothbrush in half, want the plastic to snap directly in my mouth. How sore would it be to gore the gum? Pierce the cheek. Like making a prison shank. And, guess what? There ain't no screws around. I could if I wanted to. I could do anything.

She was livid; first time I genuinely saw her suffering deep pain. Crying. Her face blotchy with gunky make-up streaks. She must've been sobbing since reading what they wrote about her. And maybe some of it was true. Truth hurts; no danger, it hurts. But we were conkers, weren't we? Pure hard nuts, solid exteriors; at least that's what I thought at the time, that's why I didn't feel guilty or try to fix her. She was a scrapper who could dig herself out of any ditch. But conkers eventually crack; why couldn't I have seen that then?

Fucking fruitcake!

She let rip at everyone from the edge of my bed, rabbited everything out. I gave her time and space. See, I *was* a good pal! I even switched the John Grant tunes off cos he sang about heart-splitting break-ups and meeting dickheads. Didn't want Moya honing into those lyrics.

If I could be zapped back, Moya, I'd hold you tight. Just the two of us again, unbreakable conkers.

I know you would, Mags. I know you would. Don't cry.

My mouth throbs. Gums and palate mainly. Tongue tastes

lethal. Bristles on the brush seem like they've been dipped in Chianti. I hold it under the water. Rinse until it returns to perfection. I bend to the tap, suck water into my mouth. Swirl. Spit. Again and again until I see clear liquid escaping down the plughole. Tap the tap with my teeth. I could, couldn't I? I could bite it. Eat it. Champ down on it. Pure crack all the enamel.

I dry my face with a musty towel. Knuckle-dry my eyes too. *What was happening inside you that night?* I had no idea, not one iota. I stare at my face in the mirror.

Why did you choose him, Moya?

Did you think he was a total rocket as well?

Erm …

I mean, from the start?

And when I see her now, she's in that same position. Eyes all over me, her hand on my knee. She wants her answer. She's still waiting for it. Basically, she wants to know if I knew it had been happening. If I knew everyone was roasting her behind her back; if I knew her MOT couldn't keep his perv paws off little floozies.

Course I knew, we both did.

I'd always known.

But it was all just gossip and rumour. Until it wasn't.

Part of me didn't want to be dragged into Moya's crap.

I lean closer to the mirror. Breathe on it. Could draw a love heart … if I gave a shit. I say it out loud: 'It had nothing to do with me, Moya.'

Yes,

I'll cuddle you,

stroke your hair,

kiss your head,

tell you how beautiful you are, that there's plenty more fish in the sea.

I'll do all that, no problem.

But don't ask me what I think about those comments. I'm immune to your heart being trampled over. It's not my fault it took you ages to realise what complete dicks they were. My job's not to untangle your brain, girl. If I spout the God's honest, you'd blame me for keeping schtum about it. You're having a hernia if you think I'm taking any blame for your psycho choices in the man department. No way, Moya; I've got enough on my plate without this.

'Did you know, Mags?'

'Not everything they were saying.'

'But how did I not know, eh? How did I not know?'

'You do now. Don't pure beat yourself up about it. He's the one to blame here, not you.'

'Feel like the whole town's pissing themselves laughing at me.'

'Don't sweat it, they were doing that anyway,' I went, trying to spray laughter into the atmos. She didn't take the bait; cut me a look that could've seared skin. 'I'm kidding, Moya. I'm kidding.'

'Not the time for jokes here, Mags. It's OK for you – you've got a future to look forward to. I'm never escaping this hell-hole of a town.'

'Course you are.'

'And you'll meet a decent guy and never come back.'

'Hope so.'

'Don't say that. Don't ever say that.'

'I'm joking. God, chill.'

She whinged about her broken spirit.

Cried more.

Full-on gush.

Seeing her tears should've set an alarm off in me; she never cried. By that stage I'd muted the alarm though.

I remember when she went to clean up her misery in the toilet I chucked John Grant back on again. Played 'It's Easier'. Really loud, hoping the words *would* rattle her eardrums, but she barely even noticed the music had changed when she returned.

And now I'm standing here in the same toilet, trying to imagine what she was doing that night. Peeing? Washing? Crying? Everything?

My head's hissing; I have to lie down. So, I do, right here where I am; cool tiles on the toilet floor stroke my cheek, glorious.

I dig my nails into my love handles, pinching and nipping until soreness shoots up my neck and down to my feet. Will totally leave a mark. After that my fingers head directly for the ten-stitcher scar. A few broken scabs still cling on. I caress the rough crusty islands with my fingertips. I tease and taunt the scabs; fear for their safety.

Davis wouldn't do that, would he? I can tell he's not the type to inflict hurt upon others. He's one of the good ones. I see how he lets people breathe and express themselves around him; he doesn't need to dominate. He's not that important. It was the lack of one of these 'good ones' that caused Moya's rage, it was her failure to find some guy with kindness in his heart. See, for her, being with a fella was all about arguing and shagging. Whereas it should be all about comfort and liberation.

The colour is back on my cheeks. I remove my fingers from the scab islands. Sometimes I feel she's actually egging me on, wants me to damage my outer shell. Destroy myself, too. Cow! She totally does; I know her. It's the same pattern: every time I'm in this mindset she's perched right there on my bloody shoulder blade.

I close my eyes tight, swat my neck with my hand. Count to ten.

Please.

1

Go.

2

Away.

3

Moya.

4

I.
5
Can't.
6
Fucking.
7
Stand.
8
This.
9
Any.
10
Longer.

When I open my eyes she's gone.

No Reply

I called to see if she was getting over that twat of hers. Tried her loads. She never picked up. OK, so she cried a bit and was raging, but I wasn't pure agonising over her. I didn't suspect a thing. It's not the first place the mind goes to, is it?

I only started to worry when she blanked school altogether. She hated it like everyone else, but free dinners and somewhere warm – what's not to like?

She didn't give a shit about her exams so I guessed she was spending her days window shopping in town or trying to sneak into Cineworld. She did that. *What's she going to do now*, I thought. *Repeat next year? Sign on?*

The zoomer had her phone switched off the last time I called. I could just see her sitting in her room listening to Jess Glynne and pure seething. Cursing her abuser, and the world in general. Planning sweet revenge: graffitiing mammoth dicks on the sides of their houses or something.

You think you know someone, don't you?

Even though I was battering the books like a private-school girl, I kept trying to get hold of her. Nothing. No reply.

It's hard to think about that day. Then again, it's hard not to. My first exam was two days away; I'd my head jammed up my studious arse. No life outside study notes.

When my mobile flashed up *unknown number* my heart began swinging like a wrecking ball. Not a big fan of unknown numbers. I pressed the glowing green icon on my phone. Could've been someone from the art school I'd applied to. Be polite. No swearing. Best Maggie required.

'Hello,' I went.

'Hiya, is that Maggie?' The voice sounded serious, sad almost. I knew who it was though, which was a relief. That relief lasted half a second, replaced by a full-on blood churn and jangled organs.

'This is Maggie,' I went.

'Hiya, hen. It's Moya's Aunt Jean here.'

'Oh, hiya.'

I didn't ask how she'd got my number. Wasn't important. Nothing rude came out of my mouth.

'I'm phoning about Moya, hen.'

Straightaway I knew.

Don't ask me how, I just knew.

I could've fucking strangled her – Moya, that is.

'Has something happened?' I went.

My voice sounded like broken glass.

Moya's Aunt Jean explained everything. Every detail. I'm not sure I even heard what she said. NOT TRUE actually, cos I wouldn't have screamed at the top of my lungs otherwise, would I? My intestines wouldn't have felt as though they were being wrenched from my body. Then the whole works: tunnel vision, seeing tiny dots in the distance, dry mouth.

Blackout.

Proper blackout.

When I came to, Mum was beside me rubbing my back.

'Breathe, Maggie,' she went in a hushed tone. 'Through the nose. Through the nose.' My eyes fixed on the wall, at nothing really, but I listened to her and did what she asked. 'That's it. Long and slow. Long and slow. Good girl.' Seemed to help. 'Good girl.' She stroked my hair. 'That's it. That's better now.'

'I want to sit up,' I went.

She helped. 'Up you come. That's it.'

I nodded.

'Just keep breathing, Maggie. The way you're doing.'

I always thought that the breathing thing was a load of toss, but it helped calm me big time. My heart steadied. Mum's eyes were different. Sorrowful.

'Something to drink?'

'No.'

Her arms surrounded me; she pulled me close to her chest. I felt fragile, that my body would crack with a good hug.

'You OK?'

'Not sure really,' I went. 'Sorry.'

'You've nothing to be sorry for, Maggie.'

But I was sorry. Sorry for giving Mum the fright of her life, for her finding me sprawled on the bed like a deformed swastika. For discovering my phone on the floor with Moya's Aunt Jean saying, 'Hello, hello, hello?' over and over.

'Do you know?' Mum went. 'Did Jean tell you?'

'I think so – I didn't hear it all though. Her voice was muffled. What did she say? What did she tell you?'

Mum stretched her lips, looked away for a split.

'What did she say?'

Her chest heaved; she checked her words before speaking, choosing each one carefully. They still resonate; I'll carry them with me, my forever words. Mum had to get them spot on. She spoke. I listened. We hugged more. I didn't cry. She stroked my hair. I vomited a little soup into my mouth.

She asked if I wanted a pill to make me sleep.

'I don't need one,' I went.

She left me to sleep the pain away.

After an hour of ceiling staring, I shot up from my bed and sifted through my bag. I retrieved a manky black vest from my washing basket. Safer.

Some girl feistiness was required so I changed the music: Janis Joplin. Stronger. Appropriate.

I rummaged about the bag until I found it hiding away at the bottom. Opened. Closed. Opened. Closed. Loosened it from its stiffness.

I pressed the tip of the compass on the meaty part of my palm, near the thumb, checking its sharpness. I concentrated, awaiting my fruitcake mode to kick in and fire me up. Then I began. First time for everything and all that jazz.

And that's how this self-harming junk began. And, yes, I'm blaming Moya for it. It's all her fault. Talk about stupid, FFS.

Diet

Rule number one: don't stand looking at your mate with eyes that scream 'abandoned child'; don't disable the poor soul by forcing him to hug you; and during said hug, don't pure grind yourself into his legs.

Rule number two: never make your mate aware that you might want to ride him, even if it's a dry ride with jeans on. That's a big *might* by the way, cos I'm not even sure myself.

If you do flout these rules, know that things could become a bit edgy between you both.

At art school and during rehearsals, Davis is the same; he's not doing or saying anything that's different. It's me – I feel like a total spanner around him. Like I've humiliated myself a bit. I don't want to fancy him, but I do. I don't want to want to snog him, but he's so gorgeous. I'm trying to focus on the bastard side of his character, in the hope it cures me. Mean, if he was an alt-right misogynistic, racist Brexiteer, everything would be perfect. There's not even one sexual misdemeanour on his rap sheet. He's like a bloody nun, or a mini Ian.

Ian's only been on the scene for about a month and already I've seen changes in Mum. Her diet for a start. She's begun to eat again. Not just stuff we can afford either or the food-bank dross. No, this is weird stuff. Maybe he's buying it, who knows. So, this big-brain Ian moseys on in and fills Mum's head with health-food solutions and suddenly my pimped-up soup and stir-fry concoctions are booted into touch.

'Mum, why are you having protein powder?'

'Ian said …'

'What the hell are soy beans?'

'Ian said …'

'Dry milk? God, I'd rather wazz up my own puke.'

'Ian said …'

That's generally how our chat has become. Almost every sentence exiting her mouth has his name attached to it. Honestly, you'd swear she's pure loved up.

'Oh, Ian likes this programme …'

'Ian's been there …'

'Ian can do that …'

I no longer have to go thrust employment potentials down her gullet; she's happy to batter into them herself. My hope is that she's on a job-search mission; I can't stomach more soup. Feel like I'm swimming in it.

They go on drives. 'Drives', yeah, right; who are you trying to kid? Pub lunches. Walks. Pictures. Swimming. *Swimming!* They do loads of things together. They've even been on an overnight to some Airbnb up north. And get this, when she's due back I'm peering from behind the curtains in role-reversal fashion. She waltzes through the door, walking on this post-sex air, and I'm standing arms folded ready to give her the pure second degree. But how could I? Her face shines, eyes whiter than I've seen in yonks; giant skip in her step. Probably been at it morning AND night, double sessions; hard to get those images out of the head. It's as if she's just lost her virginity for the second time in her life. I can tell she's dying to tell someone about her night of filth. Me? Don't even ask.

Can't exactly play the bitch, thump my thighs or stamp my feet, can I? This *is* what I wanted for her. Mission complete. I can now die a Cupid legend. If Ian had turned out to be a maladjusted maltreater female-beater I'd have gone nuts. But he isn't. He is OK. No, better than OK, he's a cool guy. A teacher, but I don't hold that against him. When we speak, his chat isn't full of all this oh-please-like-me-I'm-really-a-great-guy-when-you-get-to-know-me stuff as if he's trying too hard. He's calm and sorted and kind. Kindness; that's all you can ask of a person really, isn't it?

When we first met he didn't even hate me for catfishing him:

'So, you're Maggie,' he went. 'Or shall I call you Cilla Black?'

'Er, no, Maggie is fine.'

Mum laughed.

I had to Google that Cilla Black woman.

I laughed.

Me and Ian chat as normal folk would, not too boring. He's funny without ramming joke after joke down my throat. And he knows his music. We have loads of confabs about tunes and bands. What's good. What's shit. What makes us want to pop our eardrums. We're basically on the same wavelength tune-wise, which helped smash the ice. The best thing though – nails it for me – is that he loves the Smiths. A real fan as well. Not some pretend knob who likes them for ten minutes cos they've heard on 6 Music that the Smiths are still cool and relevant. Isn't his style. He's got all their original seven-inch vinyl and some rare imports. I'm like, wow! No way? Says I can borrow them anytime cos 'the listening experience is breathtakingly different'. No turntable though.

I know I've done the right thing by Mum. Let's be honest, if Ian can get on with me he can get on with anyone.

Not sure if they consider themselves to be bf and gf; maybe they're too old for those labels. I don't ask. Sometimes I see their hands brushing each other's; it's gentle. He enjoys doing things for her, making her happy, and I like knowing she's recovering.

I can tell you one thing though: Ian's funky dietary ideas don't extend to my plate. No danger! Can't see myself munching on nuts, mangoes or quinoa, whatever that is.

Visit

We don't argue about it; nothing to argue about. Just think it's unfair. Weird even. Not once does Mum ever ask me to accompany her to her doctor's appointment. Whereas if it were me she'd be all over it; sniffer dog on heat.

'You'll be bored out of your tree, Maggie,' she goes.

She's not wrong.

Watching people plagued by misery isn't exactly my bag, but I want to give her moral support and all that.

'I don't mind,' I go, cos I could be that person she leans her head against afterwards. But Miss Independence is having none of it.

'It's just a meeting about how things are developing. It's nothing serious.'

'Fine.'

But it isn't fine. I don't want to make the same mistake I

made with Moya: push her away, let her deal with it on her own, call me when things perk up. With Mum that won't be happening.

What annoys me is that golden balls Ian's taking her to her appointment.

'Should you not be checking if everyone's got their uniforms on?' I go.

'It's OK, Maggie,' he goes, and comedy-grins. 'I have the morning off.'

'And teachers want more dosh?' I puff.

'More money, less hours, that's what this country needs.'

'I'd be lying on the couch watching Netflix if I were you.'

He laughs.

I keep my annoyance to myself.

He gives me a lift to art school on the way to Mum's appointment so we're quids in. I sit in the back. No one speaks. Ian's eyes fix on the road. Mum looks out of the window.

The atmos confuses me. Not a we've-just-had-a-belter-of-an-argument-and-we're-not-talking atmos. You know, when the awkwardness becomes the very air you breathe. This is different. Sombre and serious. Maybe I'm thinking too much, trying to do an Anna job on it; which reminds me, I need to organise a sesh. Let's be honest, though, it could be Ian's car music that's plunging us into a catatonic state. Are Radiohead even a thing now?

Intensive care is where they took Moya.

There's a touch of the detention centre about hospitals. The reek of disinfectant, puke and food invades your nasal buds. Squeaky floors snarl at your eardrums. I remember this annoying light flickering its last goodbye when we first entered. Outside the main entrance the place was full of grotesque people smoking too many fags and munching too much grease. Scared me shitless; don't know if Mum felt the same.

She came with me to see her.

Man, talk about shitting bricks.

There are no specific visiting hours in intensive care; they gave us a time slot and told us when to come. Tough titty if we couldn't make it; think it's something to do with what type of medication the patient's being given. Everything works around their schedule. My knowledge was – and still is – zero.

We made our slot.

I pressed the buzzer below a glass window and waited. A straggly haired woman moseyed to the other side, looking as though she'd just dragged her carcass away from hours of biscuit-munching and arse-scratching. No hello. No smile. She sighed as she plonked herself down on a swivel chair. Her expression barked, 'I hate my life.' For a split I thought that maybe she was an ex-con; you know, given the responsibility of dealing with real people, being shunted slowly into society again. Don't know why I thought that, maybe she just looked like she'd throw boiling sugar over you.

'We have an appointment,' I went.

'Name?'

'I'm Maggie Yates.'

'Not *your* name, love,' she went, all sarky and superior. 'The person you're here to see.'

'Oh right, erm … Moya … Moya Burns … we're here to see Moya Burns,' I went.

She flicked some of her minging grey locks away from her forehead, scrolled her finger down a sheet of paper muttering 'Moya Burns' to herself over and over again. Definitely not a doctor.

Imagine giving this headbanger a stethoscope.

'OK, I see her,' she went. 'So, you need to go through those doors over there, go straight down to the bottom, turn left and then someone will help you.'

We headed that direction. Towards fear. Our pace was slow and considered.

'Don't mind saying, but this place gives me the heebie-jeebies.' I clung on to Mum's arm; vulnerable and needy, scared stiff.

The corridor ahead was lifeless, eerie, as if something had just kicked off or was about to; calm before the storm. You felt it.

'Just keep close to me, Maggie,' Mum went, snuggling in.

By this stage we were whispering. The unknown does that to the voice.

259

At the bottom of the corridor we found a new locked door.

Another buzzer.

It opened as we approached.

Another window.

A smiling man lifted the little latch. I did the whole name spiel again. No finger-scrolling or muttering 'Moya Burns' over and over. This guy knew who we were.

'Just take a seat over there and someone will be out to get you soon,' he went, pointing to an excuse of a waiting room to our right. No one else was waiting.

'There's a tea and coffee machine.'

He closed the window.

'I don't drink tea or coffee,' I whispered as we parked in the plastic chairs.

'You don't have to. It's not a restaurant we're in,' Mum fizzed.

I was scared.

We didn't know the state she was in yet.

The extent of the damage she'd done.

Mum rested her hand on my knee.

I put mine on top of hers.

'What do you think you'll say to her?' she went.

'Haven't a clue. Been thinking about it though.'

'Will you ask her why she did what she did?'

'Don't know. It's bonkers.'

'For some people it isn't though, Maggie. For some people

it's the only thing that'll take their pain away. The only thing that makes sense in their life.'

'Suppose.'

I shifted in my chair. Sat forward. Scratched my calf. Sat back. Puffed out my cheeks.

'You OK?'

'Yeah, just hate hospitals and the waiting.'

'It's the worst part.'

It was Mum's turn to sit forward. Shuffle. Extend her legs. Sit back again.

'Are you angry with Moya?' she went.

'Why would I be angry?'

'Because she didn't speak to you about it? She didn't tell you she was going to do … something stupid?'

'Doubt I could've done anything, even if she had.'

'You could've talked some sense into her.'

'Me? Talking sense? That's a laugh,' I went.

'Have you any idea why though?'

'Shitty few weeks. Boyfriend problems. Then she found some stuff on social media.'

'What kind of stuff?'

'Just people trying to take the piss out of her.'

I didn't want to hit Mum with the full bhuna in that moment.

'And perhaps you doing better in school than her,' Mum went, which jolted me. I took my hand off her, and seriously considered smacking it off her jaw.

'What does that mean?'

'Nothing … I didn't mean that—'

'What Moya's done has got nothing to do with me, Mum. Nothing. Got it?'

I chilled a bit, but was too annoyed to stay chilled. I turned to her again. 'No, tell me what you meant by saying that? Come on, I want to know.'

I thought she was going to melt into her chair.

'Well, she might have felt abandoned a touch, neglected even. Maybe she was jealous.'

I honestly wondered if she was talking about Moya or herself.

'That's just life,' I went.

'I agree, Maggie.'

'Mean, we can't play rebel teenagers forever, can we?'

'Thankfully, no.'

'Anyway, I've just applied to art school – no guarantees I'll get in. And I'm trying to study like a mad swot.'

'I know you are.'

'So, sorry if I've not been pure living in Moya's pocket these past few weeks. Sometimes I just need space to breathe on my own, you know?'

I felt my chest throb.

She shuffled position.

'You'll always have me,' she went.

'What're you on about?'

'If you're ever feeling alone or that things are stressing you out, remember that I'll always be here for you, Maggie. You can talk to me.' Mum's tone changed. 'You've a great future ahead of you.' She pushed her bushy brows up and down. Clown.

If I'd held her stare longer she'd have started blubbering. The eyes were already glazing over. She cupped her hand around my four fingers, squeezed them. Talk about intense. I couldn't be dealing with a blubbering mother as well as an unhinged bff; my head was totally wrecked.

As Mum came in for a cuddle a woman in scrubs popped her head inside the waiting room. Couldn't tell if she was a nurse or a doctor.

'Maggie Yates?' she went.

'Yes.' I escaped Mum's hand.

The woman scanned us.

'I'm afraid we can only allow one visitor at a time, dear.'

I gave Mum my tough-shit eyes.

'I'll wait here – it's fine,' she went.

'Sure?'

'Sure I'm sure.'

'See you in a bit then.'

I followed the woman to yet another set of doors where she extended a plastic key card from her belt, swiped it down the door's facing. As they opened inwards a swell rushed through my body, as if I'd just been syringed with a massive dose of adrenalin.

'Are you a relative?' the woman went.

'No, I'm her friend – her best friend,' I went. 'How is she?'

The woman paused, stopped walking. She seemed uncertain.

'She's still unconscious,' she went, like I should've known. 'It's mainly because of the drugs she's taken.'

'Right.'

'Don't be alarmed when you see her – all the tubes and breathing apparatus are perfectly normal.'

'Right.'

We walked in silence.

The place was stone, as if the walls and ceilings had been sedated too. Intensive care isn't really like a normal ward; beds are sectioned off by rolling curtains. But Moya had a private room. Lucky.

'How long before she wakes up?' I asked.

'We won't know at this stage.'

'Does she need an operation or anything?' Think I was beginning to piss the woman off with all my banal questions. She didn't answer; can't blame her.

'OK, here we are then.'

'This it?'

'This is it.'

'Number seventeen,' I went to myself.

'You go on in and I'll pop back around soon.'

'OK.' I watched her walk away, feet squeaking off the floor.

Swear my heart was trying to climb out of my mouth. I took a huge inhale of breath, belted out a puff before doing that knock–open simultaneous thing. Who knows why? Not as if she'd have been jumping up with a welcome hug. I even feigned a friendly smile as I entered.

Moya was on her back. Not peaceful. Mouth stuffed with a tube that was connected to some pump. Up and down. Down and up. Made a swooshing noise. Her arms were covered in drips and plasters. They'd put a wet cloth across her head and a bit of masking tape from ear to ear to hold the tubes in place. She'd a masking tape moustache. Monitors everywhere. Looked like my version of Hell. Two blue armchairs sat each side of the bed.

I almost collapsed in a heap.

This was someone else. This was a car crash lying in front of me. My eyes bunged up. Did she know I was there? A tear slid to the side of my mouth. I pulled it in with my tongue. Salty. I went to her, leaned down. Heard her.

Imagined the conversation we'd have:

Moya, it's me – it's Maggie.
Thanks for coming.
You OK, babe?
I'm glad you're here, Mags.
Anything I can do, doll?
No, I'll be fine.
I'm sorry, Moya. I'm so sorry.
Sorry for what?
I should've been there for you.
Sit your arse down.

Not as much as a flicker.

I sat down. Stared hard. Wanted to pure berate her.

Know what, Moya?

What?

It's not my fault you chose to love someone who didn't exist, is it? We were supposed to change the world together, save each other, do everything. And now look at you – you've fucked it all up. I'm so utterly sorry I was deaf to your cries. I love you with everything. Just wish you'd rise up from that bed and we could start again. If not, then just pin my broken heart to your back and take me with you. Totally mean it.

Please, Moya.

Please get up.

For me.

I wanted to draw her to me, lie beside her. Bawl her out. Cry for God knows how long.

And I did.

I did that.

Lots of salt.

Ankle

At art school people speak an octave louder than the average Joe. Lots of check-me-out volume. Why? I don't know.

Also, you can't escape the laughter; it's everywhere, all the time, nipping at the senses – every chat loaded with fake hilarity and guffawing.

In the first few weeks I was OK, but not so much now. I think everyone was on their best behaviour then, maybe in case they got cast aside for a more interesting model; someone who'd toe the social line. I thought art school would be different from high school, but it's the same crap chat: sex, internet, booze and bitching.

I see them looking at my clothes. Shoes. Hair. Make-up. Furtive little comments behind their hands. I'm not cool enough for them. Not costly enough. They don't talk art with me either; I'm not on their intellectual level. I'm just one of the art school stats from the poor part of town. Social inclusive bullshit.

Couldn't care about fitting in or being a clone; don't want to be anyone else but me. Still annoying though, so I hark back to my default: I'd take any of them in a scrap, if it came to it. No danger.

Part of it is my own fault: I'm distant, guarded. Protecting what exactly I don't know. I tell myself the only way to advance – have respect, admiration, whatever – is to work like a beast; to know more than anyone else, to be the best and most innovative designer on the course. Basically, design the shit out of them all.

The contents of my bag scatter down the stairs. Other students vault over me, eager to get to their next lecture. Bastards! Not one sinner helps pick any of my stuff up. No one helps pick *me* up. I'm not sure what happened. One minute I'm rushing down the stairs like everyone else and the next I'm flat on my tail with a throbbing ankle. A definite slip. Not premeditated. Not pushed.

I manage to drag myself to the nearest toilet. I could text Davis to come get me, but that'll only deepen the shade of my red neck. I know he would though. Even Plum or Alfie, but couldn't be doing with explaining to them how much of an awkward klutz I am.

State of you.

Thought I told you to piss off, Moya?

Well, you did, but it clearly didn't work.

Brilliant!

What happened?

I fell. Dunno. I was on my feet and then I wasn't.

You're living in a dream, Mags.

Rich coming from you.

Get up.

I can't.

No, I mean, get up. Get up, stop wasting all these opportunities.

But I thought you didn't want …

Never mind me – this is your time, Mags.

I'm trying, Moya. I'm really fucking trying.

So, try harder. Now, come on, get up.

I don't want to call, but truth is I don't know where else to turn; we don't own a car, among a host of other luxuries and essentials, and anyway, Mum's at the bloody Jobcentre. Ian wouldn't mind, would he?

'If you ever need anything, Maggie, don't hesitate to call me,' he'd told me ages ago.

'What, like money?'

'From a teacher? You joking?'

'Drugs then? That *is* a joke by the way.'

'No, like a lift to or from college, something like that. Don't hesitate, OK?'

So, he did offer. He did.

I scroll to Ian's number.

'Ian.'

'Maggie, everything all right?'

'Can you pick me up?'

'What's wrong? Is it your mum?'

'No, it's me. I just need you to pick me up. Are you free?'

'I'm free for forty minutes. Where are you?'

'Outside the art school,' I go, which is a grand lie. I'm huddled in the corner cubicle of a toilet, rubbing my ankle. Hoping Ian doesn't hear the echo and know I'm bullshitting.

'Sure you're OK?'

'Yes and no.'

'Don't move – I'll be there in ten minutes.'

I hop to the outside world, wait on my ride.

'Christ, what happened, Maggie?' Ian goes, jumping out of his car.

'Don't sweat it. I slipped down some stairs, that's all.'

'Can you walk?'

'I can hobble.'

'Here, let me help.' His arm makes its way around my back, as if I'm a war casualty.

'It's OK, I'll manage,' I go.

The magic tree hanging from his rear-view stinks. While it's more than a bit awkward just us two, I'm glad to hear Howe Gelb's voice travelling along with us. Suddenly my ankle doesn't hurt any more ... well, it does, hurts like a bastard, but you know what I mean.

'Thanks for picking me up,' I go.

'Pleasure,' he lies.

I tell him how I've made a complete eejit of myself; the images of lying in a heap of eejitness will remain forever.

'It'll be forgotten about by this time tomorrow,' he goes.

'Yeah, right.'

'It will, believe me. That sort of thing happens all the time at our school. Nobody cares after the initial piss-taking.'

I stroke my ankle.

'Swollen?' he goes.

'Like a balloon.'

I don't want to moan with the pain. I like pain, but this is not a pain of my creation, it's totally separate, like when I got my tattoo. Yeah, maybe I got that to seek out pain, trying to force it into me in a different way; zero guilt attached. I crunch my molars.

'Get some ice on to it when you get home.'

We don't have ice. Or frozen peas. In fact, the closest I'll get to an icepack is if I contort my body and shove my foot inside our empty freezer.

'Ice'll keep the swelling down.'

'Wow! You're good, Ian,' I go.

I'm glad he chuckles. He gets my humour; one of the things I like about him. But it's true – he is good.

'How was your mum this morning?'

'Don't worry, I made sure she had her kale smoothie.'

He doesn't laugh at that.

'Seriously, how was she?'

'I didn't see her – she was still in her kip.'

'She gets tearful more and more, have you noticed?'

HAVE I NOTICED?

Course I've noticed, Ian. I'm her daughter, aren't I? I live it with her. I'm the one who yanks the blinds up and pulls the curtains open, mate.

'It's the pills – they get her all emotional at times,' I go.

'That's because of …' Ian goes before stopping himself, then shoots off on the biggest tangent and starts rattling on about bands I should listen to. He thinks I'm daft.

'She's better though,' I go. 'She's working hard, I see it.'

'I'm glad to hear that, coming from you.'

I change the subject.

'Can I ask you something, Ian?'

'Sure,' he goes, probably thinking I'm about to ask him about the Manchester music scene in the early nineties. 'Ask me anything.'

'What do you see in Mum?'

'Eh?'

'Mean, I know what you see in her, but why didn't you run a mile when you met her?'

'Because she has depression?'

'Why didn't you though?'

'I don't know, Maggie. I think that—'

'Most men would've.'

'What can I say, I'm not most men,' he goes, without an ounce of sarkyness.

'I just want to understand, that's all.'

'Illness is not a character flaw, Maggie …'

'Not saying it is.'

He turns the volume down a little. Apparently that makes people think better. Or drive safer.

'I liked your mum from the moment we met. She's intelligent, easy-going, funny. She's a strong woman.'

'She's not had it easy,' I go.

'With losing her job?'

'And being a single parent. It's tough, no?'

'I think your mum has been, and is being, extremely brave, Maggie. A battler.'

'But not beautiful?'

'Oh, she is very beautiful.'

'She is,' I go.

'We seemed to hit it off, so why should I have run away?'

'Dunno.'

'There's no logic in that, is there?'

'Never really thought about it like that.'

'Sometimes those closest can't see further than the health problems because everything else has been swallowed up by them.'

'Maybe.'

'I'm sure your mum doesn't want to be defined by her illness. It's just something she has, not something she is. And something she'll come out the other side of.'

'So her depression isn't an issue for you then?' Ian puffs out his cheeks, giggles nervously.

'Listen, Maggie, I'd be lying if I said that I didn't think long and hard about it before we became close, but I've always tried to see the person inside the shell, and one thing your mother is is a good person. She can help us see the good things in life more clearly, maybe even see our own flaws and how we can alter them positively.'

'But what happens if she doesn't come out of the other side?'

'We're here now. I guess that's what we focus on.'

'Agreed,' I go. 'I'd hate her to go back ...'

'The past is the past – no one can affect it. It's impossible to even try. It can't be altered. But we can affect the here and now and the future. I think it's important to savour the moments we are in, relish them.'

'Course.'

'Look, I know you're scared, Maggie. I know you just want what's best for her.'

'I just don't want her to get hurt, that's all.'

'I'm with you on that one.'

'She's already had far too many dickheads for one lifetime.'

'I have no intention of hurting her ... I'm actually in—'

I know what he's about to say but I don't let him.

'They all say that, Ian,' I go, half joking.

'Well, you'll just need to trust me when I tell you I'm not some dickhead out to hurt your mum.'

He reaches to the dash and changes the music.

'Ever heard of Sonic Youth?' he goes.

'No.'

'You'll like them – I think they're up your street.'

The music kicks in. He cranks the volume. It's a slap in the puss. We listen in silence. He's bang on – totally right up my street.

When the car pulls up outside our gaff he turns Sonic Youth down to a murmur. I still feel the bass in my ankle. Although it's probably just the general throb.

'Maggie, for what it's worth, I think you're dealing brilliantly with what life's thrown at you.'

'What?'

'Your mum told me about your friend.'

Someone should sew her mouth up. Course she told him, course she did – it makes for great pre-sex dinner chat, doesn't it? Like using Maggie's inner demons as foreplay. Dirty sods.

'Did she?'

'And knowing your mum, I can tell where you get your strength from.'

You haven't a clue, mate.

Totally clueless.

And I don't need your judgement.

What else did she blab to you, eh?

Please tell me.

I'm trying. Every day I'm trying. So please, please don't judge me.

'I think you're pretty amazing, Maggie. And I know your mum does too.'

I don't thank him, but his comment gives me this mad rush of pride. I used to hate compliments, but now I'm like, bring them on. Shower them down.

Then when I think of the hurt I inflict upon myself that pride glides away. Did I really fall down those stairs or did something inside push me?

'You not coming in?' I go.

'Need to get back to school.'

'Well, thanks for the lift – you're a life saver.'

'Anytime. Want a hand to the door?'

'No, I'll hop the few steps.'

'Your call,' he goes.

I start hopping to the door, feeling like a complete numpty.

'Tell your mum I'll speak to her later.'

'Will do. Cheers again,' I shout over my head.

I see Mum doing a pure nosey behind the curtains; she doesn't know I've clocked her. Don't tell me she didn't make it to the Jobcentre. When I get to the door I wave; I see Ian giving her a slight head nod. They're familiar with each other now, intimate.

Mirror

I swivel Larry around with one leg (she hates that). Propel him into the air, catch him again. Sometimes I let him fall face first on to the floor. See how he likes it. No fun being chucked around, is it? No fun having someone you love discard you, is it? Not giving a toss about your feelings. Taking liberties.

Maybe if I lasso Larry around my head Moya will shoot out of him, leave me alone. Again. I loathe myself for needing her so much; she makes me feel weak cos of it.

Do you hate it, Mags? Do you? Is the place full of twats?

Why can't you just rap it?

There are some good people there too.

Who, that guy you pure fancy and that Plum thing?

Don't you see how much I'm struggling with you on my back?

Me?

Want the God's honest, Moya?

Always.

I'm too sad to enjoy it.

Yeah, sorry about that.

I miss you.

How can I tell you not to darken my door again?

Miss you too, she goes.

You could've …

Shh now. Don't.

I pick up Larry, tuck him into my bra. I need her to feel my heart; it's where she lives now.

I go to the toilet. Always a bloody toilet. FFS – might as well throw a mattress in the bath and be done with it. Mum's got the TV on full bung, would deafen an elephant.

I pluck a kirby grip out of my hair, bend it back and forth until the flimsy metal strands break in two. A weapon is born. Couple of weapons. Two knives? Blades? Shanks? Take your pick. My tights are off. I run my fingers over the scar, then over the *MY* tat on my belly and finally over my swollen ankle. Getting that tat was as sore as, man. I examine the delicate scrapes on my legs and arms, not visible to anyone else's eye, but I know where they're from. Each with its own tale to tell.

I hold up my two weapons, pick the sharpest, lob the blunt one down the bog. *Plop!* Watch it sink to the bottom. I remove every stitch except my knickers. God, I hate looking at myself in the mirror. My body demoralises me; Davis thought this too – he froze when I pressed into him. I'm lopsided and hideous. Still, it's the only one I have so I'll have to suffer it.

I raise my arms high above my head, then into the crucifix position, hunting for any evil lumps that'll transform my life. Nothing doing. All clear. A self-diagnosed picture of booby health. I don't smile or exhale relief; doesn't make me happy. I circle my nipple with the weapon ... I think about it ... I really think about it. That doesn't make me feel happy either.

You should fling that weapon away too, Maggie.

I should, shouldn't I?

I'd give everything to have her return to me. She needed me to hold her steady, to drag her up. Yet she didn't rely on me enough when her shit hit the fan. I know that now. Mean, think about it, she chose to leave cos of some prick-brained trolls and a boyfriend with a personality deficiency. And now, cos of that, I can no longer make storm with my best mate; no more howls of laughter at her antics. All I do is simmer inside.

I scrutinise: gaze at my slanted shoulders, hypnotised by my asymmetrical boobs and glacial eyes. I lift up my left boob. The other hand fixes the weapon into position. I forcefully pinch, tightening the skin, allowing veins to rise to the surface. I goad the blue canals with the weapon, this way and that. Anna's in-case-of-emergency-count-to-ten instructions enter my mind.

I count down:

10: Know the direction you're taking.

9: Be confident.

8: Dig, drag, make it quick.

7: North–south motion.

6: East of the nipple.

5: One rapid swipe.

4: You'll feel better.

Ready?

3: It'll take the pain away from your ankle.

Set?

2: Take away the pain inside too, honest.

Go!

1: Don't think too much.

Go …! Go …! Go …! Fucking go!

Afterwards I almost reconnect with some of those self-harm sites; unsure why, for advice or something. Support. It's hard, but I don't click on them.

Discovery

'Oh, sweetie, I can only imagine what you're going through,' Anna had gone in our very first session together.

Can you?

Can you really?

Can anyone?

Anyone?

Anyone!

Mistake

As soon as I opened the door I could smell it in the air. Mum was perched on the edge of her chair, no doubt figuring out how she'd break the news. Worried sick.

'Sit down, Maggie,' she went.

When any conversation begins with 'sit down', you know you're in for a massive clusterfuck.

She'd been crying.

'What is it?' I went, skin sweating. 'Mum?'

Every cell in me flip-flopped. Every sense bleary and blurred. When she spoke, all I heard was a muffled din. White noise banging my eardrums.

But I knew before she even said it.

'The pills she took put too much stress on her body, on her heart,' Mum had no misery in her voice. Complete matter of fact, as if she were telling me about the Super Noodles she'd just gobbled down. 'It was a cardiac arrest.'

Obviously, me being a dumb arse didn't know what a cardiac arrest was.

'Like a heart attack?' I went.

'Different.'

'How?'

'Her heart crashed, stopped pumping blood around her body,' she went.

'Mum, what are you …?'

'She didn't make it, Maggie.'

'Mum!'

'Her Aunt Jean called earlier to let me know.'

'But we just went to see her last week – she was only sleeping, the machines were doing all the work … she was sleeping. She was breathing. I saw her, Mum. I saw her. She wasn't stressed, she was peaceful. Her heart was going. I saw it. She was just sleeping. She just made a mistake. It's all going to get better. Mum?'

'I'm so sorry.'

'She can't have had a cardiac arrest – she was lying down.'

'That's what happened, love.' She reached out to touch me.

'She was fucking lying down.'

'She's gone, Maggie.'

To this day I still don't know the difference between a heart attack and a bloody cardiac arrest. I didn't know you could have one while asleep, or in a coma. I didn't do the whole Google search on it cos I didn't want to be broken any more.

'When did they tell you this?' I went.

'A few hours ago.'

'A few hours ago?'

I felt like belting her, chucking the toys out, yanking a scream routine from my throat.

'I didn't want to tell you on the phone.'

Those first few minutes I was numb and cold and hot and dreaming and alive. I was alive. I was the one.

Things quickly went weird; I felt a calmness stroke my body. I knew I should've been in a heap on the ground or retching my guts up, but I wasn't. Looking back, I was immersed in shock, like being submerged in water; desperately wanting to breathe but, also, trying hard not to.

'How can it be true?'

'It's true, Maggie. It's all true.'

We stared at our carpet. The well-worn pattern. I sank into our tattered couch, imagined snow falling over my head. Beautiful. Consoling.

My neck swelled with grief, but I didn't cry. I'd so many questions it was hard to prioritise.

'What time did Moya's Aunt Jean phone?' I went.

'Around half four.'

'What time did she die?'

'I didn't ask that.'

I didn't even know what I was asking, didn't register any of the replies. I was filling the space with noise and nothing else. Mean, who gave a shit what time she died? She died and that was all about it.

'It's a mistake, Mum.'

'No, it's true, love.'

'It's a mistake. Moya didn't mean anything – she didn't mean to actually die …'

'I know this is hard …'

'She was crying for help, or attention, that's all.'

'Well, of course she was.'

'She didn't mean to die.'

'I'm sure she didn't.'

'She didn't.'

'You're calmer than I thought,' Mum went.

'What do you want me to do – slash the cat? Punch holes in the walls? Sit here crying like a pure banshee? That what you want to see?'

We didn't have a cat.

'No, I just mean—'

'What's the point? What will that change? Will it make me feel better? No, it won't.'

'I agree.'

Mum returned her gaze to the carpet.

Calm?

That was a laugh.

I'd take myself out into the back garden and smash my head against the washing pole. You self-serving bitch, Maggie. You didn't even try to help Moya hunt down those pricks who abused her character, did you? You sat on your hands doing heehaw and dreaming of a life beyond her, didn't you? Admit it. It's OK, she can't hear you; she can't point the finger.

Some mate!

I'd slam my skull off that washing pole until it cracked like a coconut. I condemned her too, I did. The smug, sanctimonious me called her those things as well; it's true, I did. Told myself I was better than her, that I'd never let some guy control me the way she had, that I was too clever and astute to allow my name to be targeted like hers. That I was superior to everyone in this shithole. I abused her as much as anyone else had.

I sat there wishing I could reverse time, even just for a day. That was all I'd need to dilute the damage. One day. I'd start by telling her how much I loved her, how much she meant to me, that I was nothing without her. And to show her what a best mate was for, I would concoct a plan, a grand plan, to hunt down all those comedians who'd ever put their hands on a smartphone or computer.

But the only thing I'd control over was my head against a washing pole. That, I could achieve.

God, it was sore.

Amazing the things that go through your brain. I wondered what music would get me through it. Elliott Smith, definitely; Laura Veirs, maybe; Iron & Wine, yes. Basically, my dome was fizzing.

'I want to be alone, Mum,' I went, getting up from the couch.

'You going to be OK?'

'Think so.'

'Sure?'

I left her sitting there.

I didn't have the courage to stab or slash that night, but my right hand knew exactly what to do with itself; it had an instinctive life of its own.

I twirled and looped strands of hair around the fingers, jerked tight until I could feel my head stinging and nostrils burning. Then the weirdest thing entered my thoughts: *Maybe I'll just start speaking to her. Who'll know?*

I vowed to keep her with me, to not lose her. We could still do great things together. We could still conquer. And, when I was thinking this, Larry was on my lap, gawping up at me. This manky lamb that I'd had since I could remember was possibly going to save me.

'I'm making tea, want a cup?' Mum went, peeking her head around my door.

'That won't help.'

'Maybe we can watch something on TV?'

As if that was going to remove my aching.

'Yeah, maybe,' I went.

She squashed her lips together and left.

I heard her whistling an Elton John song while waiting for the kettle to boil. Mum slurped her tea like a gumsy old woman.

We watched *Banged Up Abroad*. I wanted to put my foot through the screen. These pair of clowns had got caught red-handed smuggling cocaine out of Peru and didn't stop whining about the shit treatment they'd received. Sympathy levels zero.

The avalanche in my head melted away.

When *Banged Up Abroad* finished, Mum turned to me. 'It's OK to cry, you know.'

'I'm too sad to cry.'

'We'll get through this.'

'Yeah.'

Grand Designs

I'm happy to spend time with Mum, doing daughter stuff, whatever that is. Mostly means sitting in the house gawking at brain-melt TV, fighting hunger pangs and listening to her munch tablets. Ian's part of this shebang as well, although I think he'd rather she was chewing cod liver oil capsules and injecting herself with goat cum instead. Pure health freak; I can't be doing with all that positivity and mindfulness guff. But, know what? Some of it is rubbing off on her. She doesn't really care too much for *Dinner Date* or *Don't Tell the Bride* these days.

'I know a place that'll be good for you, Donna,' Ian goes.

We're glued to these arrogant dickheads building dreams on *Grand Designs*. He interrupts:

'I've done a little bit of research. It could be soothing to escape the humdrum for a few days.' Mum doesn't answer;

she's staring at the stunning new build on the screen. Total house jealousy.

Ian scrolls through his phone.

'It'll be peaceful – just us sharing space with nature,' he goes.

'And you enjoy fresh air, Mum,' I go.

'Love it,' she goes.

'Who doesn't love fresh air?' Ian goes. 'It's the soul's wine.'

'I prefer Buckfast,' I go.

We all laugh.

He calls it a retreat, but we all know it's a few days of filth. 'Retreat' sounds religious, but Ian assures us it's an environment to recharge and re-engage.

'You can't put all your faith in doctors. We can try things that work in tandem with them,' he goes.

What, like eighty-three positions in a mucky weekend? I know your game, Ian.

Mum looks at his phone.

'It does look nice,' she goes.

'Eating well, thinking well, being well – what's not to like?' Ian goes as a kind of sales pitch. 'These retreats can completely detox and rejuvenate your immune system and reboot your cognitive circuit.'

'She's not a desktop, Ian,' I go.

'No, but you get the idea?' he goes.

'What do you think, Mum?'

Grand Designs has been booted into touch now that we've seen the money shot.

'I'm up for anything, Maggie,' she goes, without taking her eyes off the phone.

Don't say *that* to him, FFS.

'You should both totally go.'

She gives me a sharp sideways glance.

I park my issues until I go to bed; can't have her knowing what a bag of shit I am.

Truth: I get tight-chested and frightened when I'm not in her company. I'm trying to shake off the worry, at seeing her in the same light as Moya. I know that's not going to happen, deep down I know it, but the dark cloud is still there. It shades me.

Mum probably thinks I'm sorted, that she and Ian can simply bolt for a weekend and I'll be happy with the walls and an empty fridge. That I'll potter about for the weekend: studying, listening to tunes, rehearsing or busting Davis's chops about something that makes me want to kill him stone dead.

But other thoughts creep in, a drip-drip effect. Before you know it, you're sitting on the edge of your bed with blood on your limbs, wishing you could run away without taking anything with you, not even your name. You find yourself doing mad shit like praying to places and people you don't actually believe in, praying to the things you've previously sneered at.

I want Mum to go on a break. It's not her fault that I'm in this wind tunnel of mental fuckery.

She's not the one to blame.

Mum calls to make sure I'm not having a swinger party, prattling on about things I haven't the foggiest. Proper gobbledygook. But I try.

'You having fun?' I go.

'It's terrific – just spent a few hours in the hyperbaric chamber.'

COME AGAIN?

Helps build immune systems, apparently.

Then there's this cracker:

'And yesterday I spent the day in total silence.'

'What, no talking?'

'Nothing for the entire day.'

'Sounds … amazing.'

'It's like a deep cleansing of body and soul.'

RIGHT, CAN YOU PUT MY MUM BACK ON THE PHONE?

'I just use shower gel,' I go.

Place Ian found is somewhere up in the Highlands; got it on Groupon. Just the biz for any health-freak perv. I know his game: blast her with seeds, do a bit of heavy breathing before getting his leg over. And, all the time, so she's not allowed to speak for part of it. Bloody men!

'Practically giving it away,' he'd said.

'Are you liking it?' I ask her.

'I am. I've been thinking about things more positively. My mind seems freer,' she goes.

'Right.'

'And I've bags of energy.'

'That's great. Are you missing home?' I try not to sound like a pleading needy daughter.

'It's lovely here. I feel strong.'

'You've got to try anything, haven't you?'

'You have.'

'What's tonight?'

'There's a meditation session we're going to.'

'Sounds a hoot – can I come?'

It's bizarre having her gone; can't say I like it. I need my mum. I miss her smell, her presence. This independence lark isn't all it's cracked up to be. At least all the blinds and curtains are open and wide.

I look out of the living-room window and think about sending Davis a message. God, the gaff is so quiet. What would I write? How could I tell him that I'd love it if he came here?

Mags, I'd have a party if I were you, know that.

But you're not me.

Thankfully.

That's nice.

Well, look at you, pure misery guts.

And whose fault is that, Moya, eh?

You can't go through life blaming me for everything in your head.

No, I know.

So ...

So?

So, go buy a crate of vodka, phone up your two and a half friends and wreck this joint. Stop feeling sorry for yourself.

Sake!

Sake.

On the other side of the road some guy in a hard hat and high-vis is erecting scaffolding on the house across. He's about the same age as Mum. Random workman getting on with life, without a care in the world. I wonder if Mr Scaffolder has touched agony; if he's smelt the torture of loss. An agony and loss so traumatic that breathing becomes a chore; when you stop seeing the beauty that surrounds you, when you can no longer hear music, taste food or sleep peacefully. If so, has he ever wanted to remove his hard hat and hurl himself off the scaffold? Why can't the man outside the window have our life instead? Who's the decision maker?

A4

Anna sits muted, wondering what the hell's in front of her. It's the first session since my hush-hush visit to A & E; more than a bit mortos.

While Mum was away it hit me hard: think I need Anna more than ever. I dragged myself up. Anyway, here I am.

'Sorry for just turning up like this,' I go. 'I know I should've called beforehand.'

'You're here now,' she goes.

What, no 'sweetie'? No 'love'?

'I am.'

'And?'

My tongue won't work.

Maybe I resent Anna cos she knows too much; she knows more than anyone else does, and usually *before* everyone else does. Way I see it, she revels in knowing things; nosy old bint.

I don't mean that. Truth: I need her to know everything.

'Are you coping?' she goes.

'Yeah.'

'And art school? How are you getting on with that?'

'Fine.'

SPEAK, FFS.

'It's OK to open up.'

'I'm trying to, Anna,' I go.

I can tell I'm pissing her off. I'm pissing myself off. It's like I'm back to how I was just after the Moya thing: full of boiled blood and superiority. The leader of the don't-fucking-annoy-me brigade. Anna doesn't need me channelling this; she could end our teeth-pulling exercise at any minute.

Please, just one 'sweetie' or 'love'. Something. Anything.

She leans her eyes towards me.

'Listen, Maggie, they phoned from the hospital and asked me to come get you, remember?'

'Yeah,' I go, completely affronted now.

'We had to pretend that it wasn't a self-harming incident, but we both know the truth, don't we?'

'Yeah.' I can't look at her.

'And that's something you don't want to admit to – you'd rather we forget all about it and begin our normal banter again, true?'

'Yeah.'

My ego and pride have been completely crushed. I feel her words drill into my brain.

'It's time to address it, isn't it?'

'Don't know.'

Come on, Mags.

You shouldn't be here.

I practically live here. YOU'RE the one who shouldn't be here.

Anna seems riled; I'm thinking she's going to pull the plug on our sesh.

'Look at me, Maggie,' she goes.

She locks me in her stare.

'We kept that self-harming incident to ourselves. I didn't compromise my professionalism and I certainly didn't invite myself into knowing that information. You were reaching out and you asked for me, not the other way around. But my job is not to judge, so I won't do that. Now, unfortunately your mum is going through what she's going through, and progressing well by all accounts. She called out to me because she was worried about you – that's why I was at your house. She doesn't want everything to hit rock bottom. You've done something completely irrational and dangerous, so please do not insult my, and your own, intelligence by sitting there pretending that everything is fine when we both know that's not the case.' She leans back into her relaxed position with a get-that-right-up-you expression on her face. 'Don't we, sweetie?'

MIC DROP!

'Sorry, Anna,' I go. It's the only thing I can muster. 'I probably shouldn't have called you.'

'Who else should you have called?'

'Don't know.'

Come on, say it?

Say what?

Ghostbusters.

'Mmm.'

Never seen Anna like this; so hard, so un-Anna. Probably her true self coming out, and what I've witnessed up to this point nothing but an act. Bit like life itself. Bet she thought our sesh after the A & E incident would've been all about making breakthroughs and connections. Me clamming up has made her change tack. I'm such a disappointment.

Anna takes a sledgehammer to the silence; she bends down, picks up a pile of papers from the floor and leafs out an A4 sheet. I recognise it straightaway. The spontaneous writing I did for her. My song lyrics from ages ago. Whatever. Why hasn't she binned it?

'Now, let's talk about this, shall we?' she goes, A4 flopping about in her hand. 'It's fairly autobiographical, isn't it?'

'A little bit, yes,' I go, feeling reprimanded. 'Not all of it though.'

'I'm not here to judge. Remember that,' she goes in a judgemental tone. Then she reads, '"Girl, I'm coming to join you …"'

'You don't have to pure read it out, Anna.'

'Explain it to me.'

'It's just how I was feeling at the time,' I go. 'I wanted to

298

write a song for my band, nothing else. OK, I lied, it wasn't that spontaneous – I worked on it.'

'Do those feelings still remain, Maggie?'

'Sometimes.'

'Some of these phrases are alarming.'

'It's just creative writing really,' I go. 'A song.'

'I think what it is is honesty.'

'What's wrong with honesty?'

'Can I ask you something? You don't have to tell me, but I think truth is quite important here, as we've both conceded.'

'What?'

'Are you still harming yourself?'

I don't know what to say or how I should say it. So, I say nothing. But Anna doesn't get it; she just doesn't get it. The harming switches my mind to docile mode. Numbs me. And, one person's harming is another person's soothing. So there! Maybe the question should be: am I still soothing myself?

I brush my thighs with my index finger, not knowing how to react. I pick at my purple nail varnish until some of it falls on to my lap. I flick the flakes to the floor. She makes me feel ashamed. And I am. I hate the person I've created. But these emotions aren't present at the time of the action, are they? No, they come afterwards.

You constantly rationalise the madness you've inflicted upon yourself, trying to make sense of it, cos the thing you hate most in this life, the thing that you've no stomach for, is pain. Yet, somehow, you've managed to take great joy from embracing and enduring pain. And, know what? Deep down you understand how completely alone in the world you are, and how much of your very essence is all about self-loathing. You promise yourself you'll never do it again. You cross your heart and hope to die that you'll never do it again. You cast it aside as a one-off – a mad mental blip. Yes, that's all it was – and is. Convincing yourself that you're momentarily off-kilter, that you're not yourself and you'll soon overcome everything. Why will you overcome it all? Cos you're far too clever to get dragged into this murky world. You're bigger than that. You're destined for greater things. Colossal things. This is nothing more than an adolescent phase in your life. You'll vault over it. No danger you will. In fact, you'll have a good old laugh about it in years to come. You'll even dine out on tales of your slashing and slicing days. And, as always, you PROMISE, PROMISE, PROMISE never to do it again. But, and this is a massive BUT, when you reach into the bottomless pit of yourself, you know you'll never be able to maintain that promise. So, you go to sleep with sores, a throbbing head and stinging limbs, convinced that you're off your rocker. A certified psycho case.

I close my eyes, hoping my lids will batten down the tear hatches.

'Maggie, love?' Anna's voice is now soft and soothing. 'Is it still happening?'

'Yes,' I go, bowing my head.

'Does anyone else know? Apart from me that is?'

'Don't think so.'

'Has it intensified over the past few weeks?'

'Maybe.'

'Are you angry with Moya?'

'I'm always angry – that's why I'm here, is it not?'

'But with her specifically?'

'A little.'

'Can I ask why?'

'Cos—' I start to say before stopping myself. I feel rage rising as if it's overflowing out of the top of my head.

'Go on,' Anna goes.

'Well, cos it was a stupid thing to do, totally pointless. And for what – some tosser boyfriend and some infantile comments?'

'I see.'

'It makes me angry and upset.'

'Why?'

'Cos she was my best pal and I didn't want to see any harm come to her, that's why. That's what makes me upset. It just added to all the other shit that's going on in my life. I don't need to be dealing with that crap. It's so selfish.'

Anna delves; deep-thinking mode.

'Pointless and selfish are good words to use – hard words,' she goes. 'Does the self-harming help you process everything?'

'Helps take my mind off it.'

God, Mags, I couldn't imagine sitting through this shit.

Can I have a minute? Just one?

I stare at the floor, wipe some stubborn sleep away from my eye.

'But she's always there,' I go. I wave a hand around my head as if to demonstrate her presence.

'And that's problematic?'

'Yeah, cos I want her to leave me alone.'

'Would you say Moya's memory haunts you, Maggie?'

'She haunted me in real life as well,' I snigger. Think Anna does too.

'Then tell me why you'd like her to leave you?'

'Cos I don't want her to blame me. I see her face all the time and the look in her eyes and I think she blames me for what happened.'

'And do you blame yourself?'

'No,' I go. 'Sometimes … I don't know … it's just …' I need air; I feel like I'm swallowing a brick.

'Take your time.'

'Sometimes I think I didn't do enough, I didn't read the signs of her suffering. I was too wrapped up in my own life to care about someone else's.'

Anna touches my leg, the unblemished one.

'Look at me, Maggie.'

I don't.

'Maggie, love, look at me,' she goes, harder.

I raise my eyes to hers; everything's misty.

'It's not your fault, you hear me?'

I nod my head, without meaning to.

'You're feeling guilty, sweetie, but you've no need, and you know why you've no need?'

'No,' I sniff.

'Because it wasn't your choice – it wasn't your fault.'

I don't want to cry. I try holding it together. No use. My voice squawks.

'I can't help it, Anna. I can't help thinking that it's all my fault.'

Her face never leaves me. Her grip tightens on my leg. Then she rubs.

'Maggie, it's not your fault. Repeat it to me: it's not my fault.'

I'm on mute.

'Say it, Maggie: it's not my fault.'

'It's … not … my … fault.'

'And it's true. It's so true. No one blames you for what happened to Moya. Not one person. You shoulder no respon-sibility for it – none whatsoever. It's not your fault, OK?'

'OK.'

Anna still has the A4 in her hand. My spontaneous writing. My song. Whatever. She glances down at the words again. Lyrics. Whatever.

We pause for a well-needed breather.

She pulls a paper hanky out of the box like a magician, offers it to me. I swipe it and blow. She gives me another.

'You didn't mention any of this to Mum, did you, Anna?' I ask, pointing at the A4.

'Oh, no. What is said and done here is sacrosanct, my dear.' She raises the A4 up. 'This is between you and me.'

'Did you mention the other thing?' I go.

'Other thing?

'The … erm … the hospital thing?'

'I wouldn't do anything without your say-so.'

'I'm going to stop, Anna.'

'I really hope you do.'

'So do I,' I go.

That's the God's honest.

Totally is.

Wonder

Wonder what it would be like to hacksaw my skin.

Wonder how long I could take a naked flame on my forearm.

If I …

punched myself on the mouth,

ran my cat's claw along my gut,

put something senseless inside me,

jammed a door against my foot,

ate puke,

drank bleach.

Would anything calm me?

I want to stop, but how else can I ease the tension inside?

I want to stop, but I'd rather hurt myself than those around me.

I want to stop, but I want to feel like I exist.

I lie down on the floor. No music. Just me and my mind. Not even Larry. I crave to be swept away, so I concentrate, concentrate hard. And there it is, I've returned to intensive care; I'm walking the same rank corridors, waiting for the same doors to be unlocked, experiencing the same chill in my bones. I miss the company of Mum. But Moya only wants me. I'm the one she needs.

Boom!

There she is: face free of the cheap slap she liked to plaster on. The natural look. This Moya is fresh. So striking. So alive.

She clocks me, stands up, walks my way. I'm unsure what to do. I screw my toe into the floor, tilt my head, grimace.

Good to see you, gal pal, she goes.

You too, Moya, I go.

She throws her arms around my neck; we hold the hug for ages. I want to chin her about her crazy behaviour, but that's not something you dive into, is it? You've got to get through the 'How are you doing? You're looking great' stage first.

Wonder what would happen if I rapped my knuckles off my cheekbone two hundred times, dead fast.

How're you doing? I go.

I'm good. I'm good. Better, she goes, without taking her arms off me.

Her boobs heave up and down. I feel a bit heartless for not echoing her actions. What's the point?

You look great, I go.

At that she releases her grip.

Think so?

Totally, like Sandy from Grease *before she became fair game at the carnival.* Moya likes the analogy; she loved *Grease.* She bursts into fits before suddenly stopping.

I'm so sorry, Mags. Really, I am, she goes.

Don't apologise. You've nothing to apologise for. You've done nothing wrong.

What am I saying?

YOU'VE DONE EVERYTHING WRONG.

Wonder what it would be like to stick my head through a window?

Moya's thighs aren't exactly sticks but certainly not the thunders they were before, and her boobs are definitely a cup size smaller. She's in such good nick. The suicide diet obviously works wonders.

How's that boyf of yours? she goes.

I'm still working on it.

He seems like a keeper, Mags.

We'll see.

She wipes her face.

Don't cry, Moya.

I know all this is my fault, but I promise I won't make that mistake again. I promise. I'm crying cos they won't give me a second chance. It was a mistake. I want to return to normal. I need a second chance. Who doesn't make mistakes?

Too late, Moya.

If only you'd called me.

If only you'd called me, I wouldn't be left with this terrible longing and constant ache.

Wonder what it would be like to hover my hand over a boiling kettle.

I'm glad you came, Mags, she goes. *I really am glad you came.*

Yeah, me too.

Right, think it's time to get out of here.

She starts walking. Her pace quickens. She's a few metres in front of me. I want to shout, 'Hey, wait for me,' but I don't. I let her go. She walks through a set of double doors without being buzzed in.

And I watch.

Moya? I go.

Can she hear me? She gone?

Moya?

What?

Don't ever believe it was your fault. It'll never be.

OK, Mags. Whatever you say.

308

Wonder what it would be like to slash my wrists with some seriously graded A4.

I get up off the floor and dry my eyes, tell myself that I'm going to do it again. Everything's too tough. I need something to take the soreness away. Vow that it's going to happen again. Another ten-stitcher? Twelve?

A cracker, on the other thigh this time.

A surface slice.

Anything as long as it deadens inside.

I sit determined, visualise my muscle contracting with the force of whatever action I'm going to take. I'll do it in the toilet. Maybe while standing in the bath. Look in the cabinet for something sharp – something made for beautifying purposes – to brutalise my skin with. Tweezers could work.

I know!

I know!

I could plug Mum's hair straighteners in and use those. Two little irons. Parallel burns on my belly. That could work. Give them fifteen minutes to reach maximum heat. I open my room door.

'Mum!'

She's standing there like pure Sherlock, ear to the door, *Evil Dead* face.

'When did you get back? How long have you been there? When did you get …'

'I heard everything, Maggie.'

'What?'

I feel like collapsing right here at her feet.

'What you were saying. I thought someone was with you.'

Utter humiliation; my equivalent of a sex tape.

Mum's face changes from desperation to sadness.

I don't know why, and I hate myself for it, but I cry. Pure bawl. Directly in front of her. Pours from me, like my entire body is raining. She catches me in her arms; both of us sink to the floor. That fresh-air and wine-for-the-soul shit has well and truly vanished.

'Mum.'

'It's OK, love. It's OK. I'm here.'

'I'm so scared that you're going to do the same as her.'

When she gets us both on to the bed I fall into her. She rocks me like a baby.

'Hey, come on, Maggie.'

'I got scared when you went away. I don't want to be alone, Mum.'

'I'd never leave you alone. Never.'

She cups my face with both hands. Thumb-wipes the tears away from my cheeks. Human windscreen wiper.

'Look at me,' she goes.

I do.

'Now listen to me, Maggie, and listen good.'

I do.

'I'm not going to do what Moya has done, OK?'

'OK.'

'I'm never going to leave you. You got that?'

'Got it.'

'You couldn't count the amount of love I have for you.'

'I love you too, Mum.'

'This stuff you're going through, I wish I could take it from you, I really wish I could suck it out of your bones, but I can't.'

'And I wish I could do the same for you too.'

'I'm going to get better, Maggie. Stronger. And so are you. It's going to happen.'

'Hope so.'

'We'll always have each other, you hear me?'

'I hear you.'

She rubs the back of my head while I rub her shoulders.

'I miss my daughter,' she goes.

'I miss my mum.'

'Even the shouting mum?'

'Miss her the most.'

We laugh then release each other.

I feel my face. Bloody cheap shit mascara. Honestly, this is the last time that's going anywhere near my chops.

'I'm sorry I've been a terrible mum these past few months.'

'You're trying your best.'

'We both are.'

'Yeah.'

'Maybe we could watch some telly – that might be nice.'

'I'd like that,' I go.

'It's a plan then,' she goes.

'It's a plan.'

She recorded like seven weeks of TV while she was off hugging trees and sniffing berries.

'*Bargain Hunt* are doing a celebrity special,' she goes. 'Want to watch that?'

NO WAY! A CELEBRITY SPECIAL?

'Sure,' I go. 'I don't mind.'

She doesn't sit in her usual chair, she plonks herself beside me. Our knees touch. If I wanted I could swing mine over hers. She could take my hand and kiss it. But she doesn't reach for my hand, she strokes my hair, gently rubbing my temple with her thumb.

'I'm glad you're home,' I go.

'Me too.'

'And glad you had a good time.'

'I always thought you'd beautiful hair,' she goes, leaning over to kiss my head.

'It's a pure mess.'

'I much preferred yours to mine. Always did.'

I blow some wispy strands of hair away from her ear. She's got a new hairdo; makes her look elegant and classy, especially when she brushes it into a side pattern. She looks sexy and sophisticated. *Sexy* and *sophisticated*? Two words I'd have never put together a few weeks ago.

'How's your band doing?' Mum goes. 'I haven't asked for ages.'

'Not sure – don't think I'm good enough for them.'

'Did something happen?'

'Nothing specific, just feel I'm crap.'

'Want to tell me?'

'Well, for one, I kind of like our bass player.'

'Davis, who was here?'

'Yeah.'

'Does he feel the same?'

'Not sure. I haven't asked him and he hasn't said anything to me. It's a bit confusing.'

'Is that the reason you don't want to be in the band any more?'

'I can't deal with rejection.'

'Have you spoken with him about how you feel?'

'No.'

'Well, before you hang your mic up I'd suggest you try to have a chat with him.'

'Suppose.'

'What are you called again?'

'The Damp.'

'The Damp,' she goes, letting it swirl.

'Yeah, we might change it.'

'Know what?'

'What?'

'It's good you're doing something you love outside all this, Maggie.'

'But we're dealing well, aren't we?'

'We are.'

'Mum? We are, aren't we?'

'I know everything's been about my feelings – don't think I don't know that …'

'Everything's getting to where it should be,' I go.

She leans away from me. I've seen that look in her eye many times before. God, it's the return of the old mum.

'You don't need to hide any more,' she goes.

'Hide what?'

'This.' Mum's eyes flick towards my head, my hair. 'And this.' They move to my wrists. 'That's what I'm talking about, Maggie.'

RUMBLED!

Before I've a chance to say anything, to present my case, to bury my shame, Mum's arms are around my neck again and she's tugging me into her. I want to drown. I want to watch *Bargain Hunt Celebrity Special.* She doesn't mind my tears all over her shoulders.

'I didn't mean for you to find out,' I go.

'I should've noticed.'

'I just needed something else to think about, something to take the thoughts away. All I think about is people close to me dying. Every day I think about it.

'Maggie, I understand.'

We're both blubbering hard.

'I don't know what to do.' My face is sodden, probably disgusting. Mum tries to rub away some of my tears. They just get replaced by a fresh stream.

'My little Maggie.'

She kisses my head, practically squeezes it in her hands.

'You listening?' she goes.

'I'm listening.'

'I want you to remember the good things you have in life.'

'I will.'

'Promise me you'll always focus on those?'

'Promise.'

'Because everything must continue, Maggie, there's no other way – you can't go backwards. The past is the past. All you can do is look to the future. There is no other alternative than that – the future is yours.' She thumps the side of her skull. 'And this, this is just something I'll have to accept and live with, so don't you be worrying about me.'

'I'm sorry you have to.'

'Remember, there are great things ahead, great things waiting for you, Maggie Yates. You just need to reach out and grab them. Head straight for them. Because there's greatness in you.'

'Sometimes it's hard to see that.'

'I know it is. And you're not made of steel even if some-times you think you are.'

'*You* are,' I go, cos I do think Mum is pure steel. A tough cookie. If roles were reversed I'd be moan, moan, moan – morning, noon and bloody night. Not once have I heard her complain. Not once. Steel and determination, that's what she is. 'You're so strong, Mum.'

'I'm not, I can promise you that. And I'm as scared as you are. Maybe even more. But I'll get there – I'll get another job and start motoring again. And I'll keep trying until I get something.'

'It's important to try,' I go. 'Try anything.'

'Yeah, we won't roll over for them, eh?'

'Never.'

'Keep fighting until our last breath.'

'Exactly.'

Mum grins, nuzzles my cheek.

I nuzzle back.

Weird.

'Maggie?'

'What?'

'I want you to remember that if I'm ever physically not there for you, I'll always be here for you.' She pats my chest. 'Every minute of every day. Does that makes sense?'

'It does.'

'Sure?'

'Total sense.'

Exposure

Alfie and Plum are sitting like a couple of spanners – as if they've never met before. That's how their relationship rolls: lots of eye contact, strange body shuffling and oodles of silences. Not awkward for them, but try being in the middle of it. You feel like a fart in a Wendy house. Pretty adorable though. Davis drums his thighs.

'I need you,' I go.

They look at me as if that's not enough for them. They want me to pure crawl.

'We've missed lots of rehearsals,' Plum goes.

'Lots,' Alfie goes.

'Look, I'm still into it in a big way, I am,' I go. 'I'm still thinking of new songs we could do.'

'You got any?' Davis goes.

'Tons.'

They look at each other and nod, as if I'm being interviewed.

'And I've been scribbling original lyrics as well,' I go.

This impresses them.

'Really?' Davis goes.

'Yeah.'

'Brilliant.'

God, I could kiss him.

'I haven't lost interest in this, guys,' I go. 'I do want this. I do.'

'Let's do it then,' Plum goes.

God, I could kiss her too.

'Yeah, let's get plugged in,' Alfie says.

God, I could … no, not Alfie!

Their excitement warms me. I'm close to airing the fact that I almost molested our bass player in my room; don't want the Damp breaking up over sexual offences. Close, but not *that* close.

Davis is fiddling with his strings; he waves at me from behind an amp. His smile is wide. My heart's rattling like a snare. The wave turns into a thumbs up. I mean, who gives thumbs ups? Guy's brain is stunted. I return him a thumbs up too; he's not that sexy. No, he's mad beautiful. Whose brain is stunted?

We begin.

The bold Plum presents us with two tunes. Quality ones. We play around with them for over an hour. Cat Power's 'Living Proof' and Patti Smith's 'Redondo Beach' both suit my voice perfectly. Kudos to the chick with the musical appreciation, that's all I can say.

After a few aborted attempts it begins to shape up. It's obvious the lads have been practising like demons. Killing my theory that all they ever did was go gaga over internet porn. They sound like a slow, sordid beating pulse. I love it.

I concentrate on getting the words and voice in tip-top nick before I even think of trying to add moves. My days of flying around – raw energy release – are over. Time to develop a more measured approach.

I truly believe that we're a band worth listening to. All we need is to write our own tunes and get a gig or two. Then it's VEGAS, BABY!

'Think we might be ready,' Davis goes.

'For what?' Alfie asks.

'A gig,' Davis goes.

'I agree,' Plum goes.

'Erm … so do I,' Alfie says.

They all look at me, like I've the final word on the matter. It's cos I'm the one with the heavy load; shit dangling off my shoulders, the Damp's squib. I'm the one with the potential to hold them back. Lead singers can be replaced, you know, so get your shit together and make this happen, or else you'll be flying solo, Maggie.

'Yeah, I think so too,' I go.

'Also,' Davis goes, 'we probably need to start doing our own stuff.'

'I agree,' Plum says.

'Erm … so do I,' Alfie goes.

'Maggie, you said you have lyrics,' Plum goes.

Their six eyes assault me. Why me? What have I done? What have I got to offer? What can I present?

Lots actually.

Lots.

'Yeah,' I go. 'I do.'

Encore

After weeks of fine tuning, the Damp sound tight; proper band with proper sound.

We've been rehearsing like dogs. The idea of an actual gig jangles the old nerves, but it is time to unleash the Damp live.

When I say 'gig', what I really mean is a kind of rehearsal … with an audience. And when I say 'audience', what I actually mean is a chair in the middle of the room with my cuddly toy perched on it. Our non-paying audience of one: Larry.

I try not to look Larry in the face when we belt out our version of 'Wave of Mutilation'. I focus on getting my vocal tone right. The others concentrate on playing. But it looks as though we're all constipated, terrified to move in case we balls it up. Petrified of anyone hearing us.

It's only Larry!

What does he know?

On 'Hotel Yorba' we crank it up, start to enjoy ourselves. Larry's feet tap, even though he probably feels like a total numpty watching us alone. When we finish, he doesn't applaud. But, still, I hear it.

That was quality. Really, it was. No joke. It was shit hot, she goes.

You're not just saying that, are you? I go.

No, honestly. Do another.

We play another.

Do you have any songs of your own? she goes.

'I think we need to play one of our own compositions,' Plum goes.

Not a word is uttered.

Feet shuffle.

Everyone looks at me.

I've prepared for this moment.

I rifle through my bag, pull out four A4 pages and hand everyone a copy. I watch them drift into their own spaces. Read. Letting the words soak in. There's a buzz of excitement in the air. I observe them pore over every syllable of my song. My stomach and spleen are jigging. Similar feeling to when Anna read it.

Davis's eyes flit between the A4 and me. Can't figure him out. Is he disappointed? Sad? Supportive? I've got it: he totally fancies the arse off me, now that he can see deep into my sonic soul. I undo my lace, tie it again, killing time until someone pipes up.

'Wow!' Davis goes, inflating his cheeks.

Shit. Please don't tell me I've buggered everything up.

'Yeah, wow!' Alfie goes.

'Profound, Maggie. Really profound,' Plum goes. 'Can I ask what inspired it?'

No, you bloody well can't, Plum. Do you see me delving into your muck? The place falls silent. They're waiting to be thrown something. I wasn't expecting this reaction. My body heats up.

Really? We're doing this now?

'Well ...' I go.

'Is this about you, Maggie?' Davis asks.

'Er ... no. It's about my friend.'

'Oh, right,' he goes.

'She was a bit of a fruitcase,' I go. 'In a good way.'

'Was?' Plum goes.

'She died.'

Their shoulders sink.

And I tell them how it happened. Tell them how brilliant and bonkers she was. Tell them that her name was Moya, that she was my best friend. Tell them how tremendous she was and how much I loved her. And always will. Tell them that there are days when easy gets harder, and days too when harder gets easy. But I'm OK. I am.

My voice maintains itself. I stand tall. Wait for a response.

'I say, let's do it!' Davis goes.

Plum adds, 'Yeah, let's do it.'

'Erm … yeah, let's,' Alfie goes.

'You lot have to come up with a tune for that,' I go.

They all nod. No bother to these guys.

Pure love my band.

Live

Backstage, Davis teases me with this rubber suicide-prevention wristband. When I say 'backstage', what I mean is a room next to the toilet with this two-seater thing everyone insists on calling a sofa.

'I'm not wearing that, Davis,' I go.

'But it means—'

'I know what it means – I can read. Still not wearing it.'

'Cos of the colour?'

'No, not cos of the colour.'

'Tell me then? I thought you'd like it.'

'Well, you thought wrong, didn't you?'

'Not even the sentiment? Mean, surely you get that?'

'I do, I'm just not putting it anywhere near my body, that's all.'

'But it's to raise awareness.'

I'm firm.

'Davis, I know what it's for, so please stop dangling it in front of my face. If you like it so much, you stick it on your wrist and you raise awareness to your tiny heart's content.'

The past few months have been my awareness. Larry has been my awareness. My hair, arms, belly and ten-stitcher have been my awareness. Let's just consider that I'm well and truly aware.

'I'll keep it in my pocket,' he goes and places the green wristband inside his jeans pocket. He tuts.

'And don't tut,' I go.

'I didn't tut.'

'You did – I heard you.'

'You heard nothing.' He does a comedy Pinocchio nose pull; makes me chuckle, girly style. I try to boot him. Miss. My kick attempt reaches about ten centimetres off the ground. I try to slap him. Miss. He catches my hand, we link our fingers together and we don't pull them apart.

'Right, I'm going to do some vocal exercises,' I say, and head to the manky bog. 'You turn your knobs or tighten your strings or whatever you do.'

When I saw the flyer *WANTED: BANDS*, I suggested we play at it. It was for some mental health charity or other, but that's not why. It was cos the art school was hosting. It was our time to step up and shine. I made the call.

Maggie Yates secured a twenty-minute set for a band

nobody had heard of. Aren't I pretty impressive? Pretty terrifying. When I told the rest we had a gig, a gig where people would actually watch and be entertained, they all sat in stony silence, pure funeral-faced. Practically smelt the shit running down their legs.

Oh, this is happening.

Worst part of Mum climbing out of her pit? She declared the need to 'see her little girl perform' and that she and Ian would be coming: proud parent versus the daughter with the red neck. God, parents can be a pure noose sometimes, can't they?

I see them standing near the side of the stage, trying not to be seen, sticking out like a pair of fogeys who've forgotten their age, or opened the wrong door somewhere. The tall, slender chick with the China-doll face looks amazing though. All the male students totally MILF drool into their cider at her. My mum. Ian's arm scoops around her waist as if they're at a Coldplay concert. Honestly, talk about choking your street cred.

Since I'm the one studying fashion and textile design and managed to pull an A in my latest assignment – an *A* thank you very much … Applause! – I take it upon myself to be the Damp's stylist. Little bit of advice here, little bit of tweaking there.

Alfie wears a pork-pie hat with a shirt and tie combo. Sounds awful, but the boy looks the part: mad fresh drummer. Davis bought himself a pair of Diadora high-tops, similar to my Adidas ones but nowhere near as cool. How could they be? He buttons his tartan shirt up to the neck and lets it hang over his skinny jeans. I gel up his hair and slick it back. Total sex god! Yeah, in his dreams. Still, I'd fancy him to death if I saw him pluck that bass. What am I saying? I do fancy him to death. Plum's rocking this cracking purple sixties minidress, locks backcombed to give it that electric-shock state. Wild and stunning. Goodbye, Miss Prissy Drawers; hello, Miss Foxy Knicks. I'm not joking when I say she could've easily passed as a sexier version of Björk or PJ Harvey. Me, I wear dogtooth trousers, delighted they fit. I've hung braces off them for that extra lead-singer effect, sprayed some second-hand Docs metallic blue and chucked my *Queen Is Dead* T-shirt on. Best part is that I got my hair cut into a bob, Karen-O style. It's shiny and alive. Chuffed it's grown back. Mum yapped on and on about me getting it cut; she prefers it longer. Totally nagged me about something so insignificant; mean, come on, screw the nut, Mum. Got to laugh though. Ian likes my new hairdo; he's sound. The man understands music and image go together like cancer and chemo.

We decide to kick off with the song I wrote the lyrics for. Followed by Davis's tune, called 'Revolution in My Hole'. Then we'll hit them with a couple of covers, before ending in Plum and Alfie's composition, 'Pleasures in the Afternoon'. Dirty devils.

Right, I want you to go out there and boot these posh twats where it hurts. Play something banging, she goes.

I'm glad she's with me; I guess she always will be. I will not be afraid of the M word any more.

When they announce us on stage I swear I need a nappy to hold me together. I see loads of folk from my course, waiting, wondering and muttering. I see Mum and Ian canoodling.

After a beat, I welcome their smiles; I hear their applause. I sense their enthusiasm and support.

I lean towards the mic, adjust it a little and open my lungs. Scream:

'We're the Damp. This song's called "Follow You Down".'

An onslaught of whoops!

I turn to the lads. Alfie salutes me, Plum gives me a go-sister nod and Davis blows me a kiss. My heart!

'One, two, three, four.'

And we play it.

We play it loud.

Follow You Down

Girl, I'm coming to join you where lights don't glance,
Gonna follow you down to Hades' dance,

Where we'll dance demons away, let other voices fade,
If I follow you down we'll revive our crusade.

Yet I last in this hollow, thoughts I have to purge,
I'll wait to follow you down, when once again we'll surge.

So, my fearsome friend, ask time to stand still,
Until I follow you down where we'll share a thousand thrills.

Sleep sound, beautiful you, bathed in eternal rest,
Never will I rip your light, your love, from this broken chest.

Your light, your love, from this broken chest.

Curtains

She's in her chair but the TV is off. A breeze catches the new curtain and blows it back towards us: a sail without a ship. As the wind hits her face, she sucks the gust through her nose, grins gently and flutters her eyes. She flips a page of her book at the same time as I do with mine. When her phone pings she actually laughs out loud at the message.

Message

My music is switched off for a change. I think of shooting the breeze with Larry, lift him to me and blow a little wind on to his face, suck in his stench. I imagine him grinning gently and fluttering his eyes. God, imagine if he could. But I've no need for Larry to keep me afloat. I place him on the shelf where he belongs. He gets the message.

EPILOGUE

Needle

Can't believe I'm back in this place again.

How many times have I promised to be done with all this teenage-angst crap? Lost count. But when the pain's gone you forget how sore it was, or the psychological effort it takes to actually carry it out. That's the last thing on your mind. You visualise the fruits of it on your body; totally warms my glow. Comforting even. A sense of achievement. A lifelong buddy. That's when you know it's got hold of you and you've caught the bug.

It's hard to share with those who've never tried it, who haven't experienced the relief and exhilaration when it's over. Pointless trying to make those who aren't into it understand. They'll never get it.

When the throbbing stops and the scabs fall off, the first thing you want to do is jump straight back on that merry-go-round and have another go, find a fertile patch and hammer your stamp on it. I honestly believe it's like being part of some sordid little club. Now, you tell me, is that a sure sign of a fruitcase or what?

I don't take my eyes off the needle for one second. Totally transfixed. I follow as it slowly edges towards me. My head buzzes, too. When it touches my skin I drop my eyelids and plead with it to weave its magic. Sharp, powerful, permanent. My tiny tormentor. This modest spike has me at its mercy, big time. Has me almost begging for it. I feel like a pure slave to its clout.

I'm lying down, pinned to a bed, no chance of escape; there's nowhere to go. And, besides, I don't want to free myself. This is what I've become. Who I am.

Mustn't tell anyone.

No one must know.

Still, I guess Davis will see, won't he?

When needle stabs flesh, my body tenses, toes stiffen. I keep those lids closed and allow it to ravage me. If I think about it too much I'll cry and that's the last thing I want, so shutting the mind down prevents tears.

God, I've missed the sensation of liquid running down my belly.

Trickling.

Tickling.

Teasing.

After being without it for so long, it's exactly what I need.

What I've longed for. This is my time. Again.

When it's over, I sit up, examine the damage. Nice job. Perfect in fact. The guy's tattooed the letters O and A either side of the Y on my existing MY tat.

I think she would've liked it.

She would've, wouldn't she?

She does, Mags. She does.

Acknowledgements

I'd like to thank the following people:

My editor, Hannah Sandford, who guided me through the process: your kindness, patience and creativity made this a true collaborative experience.

My agent, Nicola Barr, for indulging my abundance of farcical book ideas and reminding me that structure is vitally important. Your unwavering support is a huge comfort.

I'll forever be indebted to the greatness of Sarah Crossan, who read early drafts of *The M Word* in the days when it had an altogether ridiculous title, and provided me with such thoughtful and considered feedback. Thank you.

The brilliant Bloomsbury team, who continue to champion and support my work.

My parents, John and Rosaleen, for it all.

About the Author

Brian Conaghan was born and raised in the Scottish town of Coatbridge. He has a Master of Letters in Creative Writing from the University of Glasgow. For many years Brian worked as a teacher and taught in Scotland, Italy and Ireland. His first YA novel for Bloomsbury, *When Mr Dog Bites*, was shortlisted for the 2015 CILIP Carnegie Medal, and his second, *The Bombs That Brought Us Together*, won the 2016 Costa Children's Book Award. *We Come Apart*, a verse novel co-authored with Carnegie Medal-winner Sarah Crossan, won the 2018 UKLA Book Award, and his fourth novel, *The Weight of a Thousand Feathers*, won the 2018 Irish Book Award for Teen/Young Adult Book of the Year.

@BrianConaghan

HAVE YOU READ

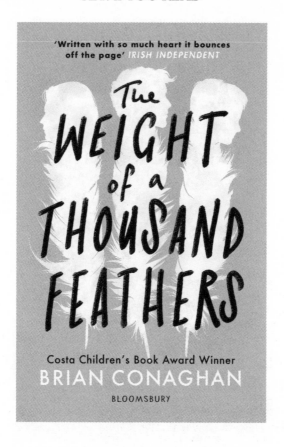

AN POST IRISH BOOK AWARDS

TEEN/YOUNG ADULT BOOK OF THE YEAR 2018

'Help me,' she says. She's clear-eyed and steadfast. 'Please?'

How far would you go for someone you love? What would you do if they asked? When Bobby Seed's mum asks him the Impossible Question, how will he answer?

'Conaghan is a sublime storyteller'
The Times

OR THE BRILLIANT

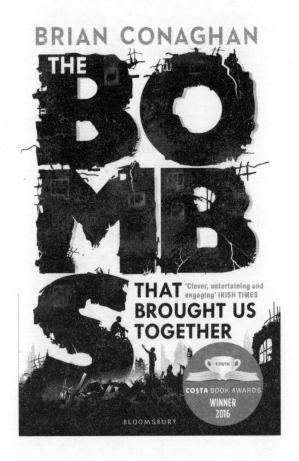

BRIAN CONAGHAN

THE BOMBS

THAT BROUGHT US TOGETHER

'Clever, entertaining and engaging' IRISH TIMES

COSTA BOOK AWARDS WINNER 2016

BLOOMSBURY

WINNER OF THE COSTA CHILDREN'S BOOK AWARD 2016

Charlie Law has lived in Little Town all his life and he knows the rules. The most important of which is to never to get on the wrong side of the people who run Little Town. But when he meets Pavel Duda, a refugee, rules start to get broken. Then the bombs come, and the soldiers, and Little Town changes for ever …

'A dark, powerful tale of survival, morality and loyalty'
Scotsman

a story about life, death, love, sex and swearing

'Funny, foul-mouthed, fantastic'
CHARLIE HIGSON

when
$#!+!
mr dog
**$€!
bites

SHORTLISTED CILIP Carnegie Medal 2015

brian conaghan

BLOOMSBURY

SHORTLISTED FOR THE CILIP CARNEGIE MEDAL 2015

A routine visit to the hospital turns sixteen-year-old Tourette's sufferer Dylan's life topsy-turvy. He discovers that he's going to die next March. It's only August, but still – he has THINGS TO DO. So he makes a list – *Cool Things To Do Before I Cack It* – and sets out to make his wishes come true.

'So surprising and charming it would be hard not to feel a little uplifted'
Observer